'He's not f

She frowned up
that?'

'I mean you wouldn't be happy married to a man like Robert. What's more, you'd end up making him miserable.' He smiled. 'With all that spark and drive in you, you'd eat him alive in time.'

'No one said I was going to marry Robert,' she said coldly. 'And, even if I were, I don't see what business it is of yours.'

Dear Reader

Easter is upon us, and with it our thoughts turn to the meaning of Easter. For many, it's a time when Nature gives birth to all things, so what better way to begin a new season of love and romance than by reading some of the new authors whom we have recently introduced to our lists? Watch out for Helen Brooks, Jenny Cartwright, Liz Fielding, Sharon Kendrick and Catherine O'Connor—all of whom have books coming out this spring!

The Editor

Rosemary Hammond grew up in California, but has since lived in several other states. Rosemary and her husband have travelled extensively throughout the United States, Mexico, the Caribbean and Canada, both with and without their two sons. She enjoys gardening, music and needlework, but her greatest pleasure has always been reading. She started writing romances because she enjoyed them, but also because the mechanics of fiction fascinated her and she thought they might be something she could do.

Recent titles by the same author:

THE HOUSE ON CHARTRES STREET
ISLAND OF LOVE

LEARNING TO LOVE

BY

ROSEMARY HAMMOND

MILLS & BOON LIMITED
ETON HOUSE   18-24 PARADISE ROAD
RICHMOND   SURREY   TW9 1SR

First published in Great Britain 1993
by Mills & Boon Limited

© Rosemary Hammond 1993

Australian copyright 1993
Philippine copyright 1993
This edition 1993

ISBN 0 263 77971 8

Set in Times Roman 10½ on 12 pt.
01-9304-48046 C

Made and printed in Great Britain

CHAPTER ONE

VANESSA threw the inter-office memo down on her desk. 'I don't believe this!'

Across the small office a short, stout grey-haired woman was just shrugging into a coat. 'Don't believe what?'

'This!' Vanessa held out the offending document as though it were something the cat had dragged in. 'They're sending me a trainee. With all the other things I have on my plate, our new masters now want me to teach some moron the ins and outs of running the trucking business.'

She ran a hand over her sleek black hair in exasperation, loosening the heavy coil at the back of her neck. Then she snatched the horn-rimmed glasses off her nose and began polishing them furiously with the hem of her heavy cotton shirt.

'Well, we don't know he's a moron, do we, Vanessa?' her aunt asked equably.

Vanessa glared at her. It was all her fault. What had possessed the woman to sell what had been a comfortable family trucking business for two generations to a huge international conglomerate that would only eat them alive? They'd been over it a hundred times, both before and after the take-over, and got exactly nowhere.

'Well, he has to be, doesn't he?' Vanessa grumbled. 'Why else would they ask a small outfit like ours to train him? Oh, Aunt Harriet, it may not be too late. We could still put Robert or one of the other company lawyers on it and break that agreement. They couldn't hold you to it if you pleaded temporary insanity or something.'

'Don't start, Vanessa,' Harriet said in a warning tone. 'I've given you my reasons for selling so many times I've lost count. I can't handle the business alone any more. I want to retire. I need the money. It's done, my dear, and I'm not going to change my mind. Let it go.'

'Well, I could handle it!' Vanessa blurted. 'I know it inside and out.'

'My dear, of course you could handle it. But you're not going to be here forever. One day you'll want to marry, have children and leave all this.' She sighed. 'If only Howard and I had had a son.'

Vanessa clamped her back teeth together so she wouldn't scream out loud. It was the same old story, and there was no point getting into another argument. Harriet was of the generation that had got left behind by the whole feminist movement, and nothing she could say was going to change that.

Vanessa loved her aunt, her only living relative, but her hidebound ideas about the roles of men and women were carved in stone. It was as though time had just stopped for her around 1960.

According to Harriet's deepest convictions, a woman worked at a job only until she married, and that was the end of her career, her life in the world.

From then on her whole existence centred around making a man happy, caring for a home, children, with all the boring drudgery that entailed.

Never mind that she'd stepped in when her Uncle Howard died a year ago and kept the business running smoothly. Never mind that she'd worked there since she was in school, manning the dispatch office, helping negotiate union contracts. She even knew how to drive the great beasts herself. Harriet had it indelibly fixed in her mind that the moment Mr Right came along she'd leave it all in a flash.

'When is he coming?' Harriet asked timidly now. 'The new man?'

Vanessa snatched up the hateful memo, gave it a cursory glance then crumpled it in her hand. 'Today,' she snapped. 'In fact, he's due any minute.' She jumped to her feet. 'And I still have to juggle the week's assignments. As usual, every one of our regular drivers wants Christmas week off, and now I've had this millstone hung around my neck.'

'What's the millstone's name?' Harriet asked.

Vanessa darted her aunt a suspicious look, catching the hint of an amused smile on her round, innocent face. 'Oh, I don't know. What difference does it make?' She smoothed out the memo and held it up. 'Rees Malory,' she read aloud. She threw the memo down. 'What kind of name is that?'

'Well, I think it's a rather nice name.'

Just then there came a light tapping on the glass panel of the door into the corridor. It opened, a dark head appeared, and a tall man stepped inside. He stood there for a moment, glancing from one woman to the other, then smiled and walked over to Harriet, his hand outstretched.

'How do you do?' he said. 'You must be Mrs Farnham, my new boss. I'm Rees Malory.'

Harriet stood glued to the spot as though mesmerised, gazing with glazed eyes up at the man who stood there, towering over her. 'I'm afraid not,' she murmured, holding out a limp hand. 'You want my niece. *Miss* Farnham, that is. She's the one in charge here.' She laughed giddily. 'I'm only the silent partner. Vanessa runs the business.'

Vanessa had cringed at Harriet's emphasis on the 'Miss', knowing full well what diabolical plot had started hatching in her mind the moment she set eyes on the tall man. Inspecting him closely now as he chatted with Harriet, she had to admit there was something about him, a sort of presence, that shattered her expectations. He didn't look at all like a moron, and vague suspicions began to dance around in her head. Had he been sent here to spy on her? Or, worse, to take over her job?

He looked to be in his late thirties, past his first youth, with an air of experience and authority about him that was hard to define. Also there was no denying the fact that he was a very good-looking man. He was wearing a perfectly tailored charcoal-grey suit, crisp white shirt and dark red tie, and carried himself well, with a graceful, easy carriage. His features were chiselled, with a firm, straight nose and strong chin, and he had a thick head of dark brown hair that shone with burnished gold highlights where the pale winter sun struck it through the window.

He was walking towards her now, smiling, his hand outstretched. '*Miss* Farnham,' he said with a slight nod of his dark head. 'I'm very pleased to meet you.'

'Mr Malory,' she murmured, looking up at him.

His eyes were a peculiar deep blue-green colour that seemed to change from a slatey near-grey to a brilliant emerald as he moved from the shadows into the light. She took his hand, shook it briefly, then dropped it like a hot coal, reminding herself sternly that, however attractive he might be, this man was the enemy.

He put his hands in the pockets of his trousers and glanced around the small, untidy office with an air of confidence that bordered on arrogance, his gimlet eyes darting about as though searching for flaws and shortcomings in its décor. As she watched him, Vanessa was struck with the sudden knowledge that Rees Malory was the kind of man who would instantly take over if she let him. It was time to assert her authority.

'The memo I received from the head office says that you're here to be trained in the trucking business,' she said in a loud, firm voice.

'Yes. That's my understanding. Orders from on high, you know. Just like you.'

She placed her hands flat on the top of her desk and leaned over it. 'Well, tell me, what do you know about it?'

He gave her a quick, practised smile, obviously meant to be disarming. 'Not much, I'm afraid. That's what I'm here for, according to the powers that be, to learn from you.'

Definitely not disarmed, she folded her arms across her chest. 'Where have you worked before this?'

'Oh, lots of places. I've been with the company for several years. They move me around quite a bit, rather a rolling stone.' He flashed her another smile. 'I guess you could call me kind of a trouble-shooter.'

'There's no trouble at Farnham Trucking that I know of,' she said evenly.

'I'm sure there isn't.' He took a step closer to her and frowned down at her. 'Look, Miss Farnham, I'm not here to cause trouble for you or try to find flaws in your management. The trucking business is a fairly new enterprise for the company, and since I happened to be available they thought I should learn more about it. That's all.'

'Well, Mr Malory, I'm very busy right now and not really interested in the company's long-range plans. Have you checked in with Personnel?'

'No, not yet. I wanted to meet you first.'

'Well, I think you'd better do that now. I have an urgent matter to deal with and won't be able to spend much time with you today. Our new masters have seen fit to saddle us with about a hundred forms to fill out, and I imagine that will keep you busy most of the day anyway.'

'All right,' he said. He started towards the door, but turned around before opening it. 'Tell me,' he said, 'what's the problem that's so urgent?'

'Oh, the usual one around this time of year. I need someone to drive the Portland run the day after Christmas, and none of my regular drivers wants to take it.' She laughed. 'I may end up driving it myself.'

His eyes widened. 'Can you?'

'Sure.' Suddenly a devilish idea popped into her mind and she gave him a deceptively pleasant smile. 'I don't suppose you'd like to take it? Since you're here to learn the business.'

His eyes narrowed at her, and she felt a thrill of intense satisfaction at his obvious discomfiture. That ought to put you in your place, Mr Malory, she thought, and waited to see how he would manage to wriggle out of it.

'Of course,' he said blandly. 'I'd be glad to.'

Her mouth fell open. 'What makes you think you could handle one of our rigs?'

'Well, I've driven lots of trucks. I'm sure I could learn.'

'You'd need a trucker's licence in the state of Oregon.'

He shrugged. 'Then I'll just have to get one, won't I?' With a little salute, he went out through the door.

When he was gone there was dead silence in the room. So absorbed had she been in the tense little contretemps with Rees Malory that Vanessa had forgotten Harriet was still there until she cleared her throat loudly.

Vanessa darted her a quick glance. 'Well?'

Harriet smiled. 'So that's the moron, the millstone round your neck.' She sighed. 'I should have such a millstone.' She darted a sly look at her niece. 'Lucky you,' she said, then busily buttoned up her coat and set her hat on her head.

Vanessa gave her a withering glance. 'You can't be serious. And don't think I'm not well aware of what's going on in that devious mind of yours.'

Harriet raised innocent eyes. 'Whatever on earth do you mean?'

'I noticed you were pretty quick off the mark to let him know I wasn't married. *Miss* Farnham, indeed! If you've got any matchmaking schemes under that hat of yours, you can just forget them right now.'

Harriet made a clicking sound with her tongue. 'That's a terrible attitude for a young woman to have!' she said, shocked. Her eyes swept over her niece from head to toe in frank appraisal. 'And while we're on the subject, you'll be a spinster forever if you don't do something about your appearance.'

'What's wrong with my appearance?'

Her aunt waved a hand in the air. 'Look at you! A pretty girl like you, all that beautiful hair pushed into that awful bun, those hideous glasses, a perfectly good figure hidden behind those baggy old trousers and shapeless sweaters. 'Why,' she finished up indignantly, 'you'd have to look twice to know you're a woman at all.'

Vanessa laughed. 'I think you might do the same if you spent your whole working day surrounded by rough truckers.'

'Rees Malory is definitely *not* a rough trucker. And you can't tell me you're not just a tiny bit attracted to him.'

Vanessa laughed. 'Oh, yes I can. And, believe me, even if such a stupid thing did enter my head I'd nip it in the bud long before it had a chance to blossom.'

'Would you please tell me why?'

'Well, for one thing, I don't trust him. I mean, why is he here?'

'To learn the trucking business.'

'So he says.'

Harriet eyed her carefully. 'There's more to it than that, isn't there?'

'Of course not.'

'Yes, there is.' She thought a minute. 'He doesn't look married, and I didn't see a ring.'

'And I'm sure you looked,' Vanessa said drily.

'You know, he reminds me of someone, but I can't think who. Must be a film star.' Harriet closed her eyes and wrinkled her forehead, pondering. Then her eyes flew open. 'I know. It's David Milford!' she exclaimed triumphantly. 'The colouring is different, but they're much the same. You know, the way they carry themselves, that certain air of confidence about them. And, of course, they're both very handsome men. Yes, he's much like David.'

'You think so?' Vanessa said. 'I hadn't noticed.'

'I don't believe you. Now, look here, Vanessa, you're not going to let one bad experience with a man spoil your whole life, are you?'

Vanessa leaned across the desk and gave her aunt a baleful look. 'What you will not understand, Auntie, dear, is that I don't see my life as lacking in anything. I'm perfectly content with it just as it is.' She stood up straight. 'Now, as I recall, you were just leaving, and I've still got to find someone to take that Portland run next week.'

'I thought Rees Malory volunteered.'

Vanessa made a wry face. 'Oh, I don't for a minute expect him to show up. That was just smoke. Male vanity. They'll never admit they can't do one blessed thing.'

Harried sighed deeply. 'Oh, my dear, I hate to see you turning into a man-hater. I mean, feminism is all well and good, but you can't just wipe out fifty per cent of the population because one man——'

'Aunt Harriet!' Vanessa said in a warning tone.

'All right, all right,' she said, snatching up her handbag. 'I'm going.'

'Besides, I don't hate men. How could I when I work with them closely all day? I get along quite well with all the drivers.'

'Yes, because you've brainwashed them into thinking you're not a woman at all.'

'Aren't you forgetting Robert?' Vanessa asked defensively.

'Oh, Robert,' Harriet said with a dismissive wave of her hand.

Vanessa had to laugh. 'Well, he's a man, isn't he? I go out with him, don't I? Who knows? I might even end up marrying him.'

'Hah! If you did, I'd pity poor Robert. No, my girl. Nice as he is and much as I've relied on his legal help, he's no match for you.' The mild grey eyes gleamed. 'Now, Rees Malory——'

'As far as Mr Malory is concerned,' Vanessa broke in sharply, 'I intend to teach the man what he needs to know about the business as quickly as I can, then get rid of him, hopefully for good.'

'Yes, Vanessa,' said her aunt sweetly. 'However,' she added as she made for the door, 'you may not find that quite so simple as you think.'

'Goodbye, Harriet,' was the firm reply.

When her aunt was safely out of the door, Vanessa settled down into her chair and breathed a sigh of relief. Harriet meant well, but every time they had one of these discussions all the old wounds were ripped open, and she started bleeding all over the place again.

Harriet had been right, of course. Rees Malory was so much like David that it was uncanny. Their looks were quite different, and if the two men were to stand side by side there wouldn't really be much resemblance, except that both were unusually good-looking. Where David had been blond, this man's hair was dark. David's eyes had been a different shade of blue, without the greenish tinge, but with the same veiled devilish gleam in them.

The similarity between them was more in a certain insouciant air, the way they carried themselves with such lithe grace. David! She'd vowed never to let thoughts of him trouble her again, and now this man had come along to bring it all back. She knew it was unfair to judge him on that basis. Just because they were similar types it didn't mean their characters were identical.

After all these years the image of the great love of her live, the only man she'd ever really cared about in her entire twenty-five years, still had the power to disturb her. Even though he'd taken what he wanted from her then left her, the bitter feelings she still harboured were not so much against David as they were

16

against herself, her own stupidity, her gullibility, her romantic illusions.

She'd actually believed him when he said he loved her and wanted to marry her, trusted him so completely that when they ended up in bed together she'd assumed it was only a normal preliminary to marriage. Granted she'd only been nineteen, with no real experience of men, but she still should have known better, and she wasn't ever going to let herself be fooled like that again, not by Rees Malory, not by any man.

Nor was she going to let him take over Farnham Trucking, if that was what he had in mind. She'd fight him to the death for that. Yet even as she steeled herself for battle, she couldn't quite silence the little voice deep inside her that whispered she was in pretty bad shape if the only thing she had to fight for was a job.

She picked up the telephone and started dialling the first number on her list. She still had to find a driver for next week.

The next morning Vanessa went into the office early. She'd drawn a blank on every call she'd made yesterday so, after sending out the trucks for the day's deliveries, she sat down at her desk to start telephoning the few remaining non-union drivers she used occasionally. The union wouldn't like it if she found one, but she had no choice. That shipment to Portland had to go out on schedule.

Her best hope was Jim Lake, from Medford, but when she reached his home his wife told her he was off to Seattle on a delivery for another trucking company and wouldn't be back until Thursday.

'Well, will you please ask him to call Vanessa Farnham as soon as he gets back? It's really quite urgent.'

'Sure, Vanessa, I'll tell him, but with the weather acting up the way it has he may not get home on time.'

'I know,' Vanessa said with a sigh. 'But I'd appreciate it very much if you'd try.'

After they hung up, she tried the two remaining possibilities, but one of them was gone on long runs and wouldn't be back until after Christmas, and the other had plans to spend the holidays with his wife's family. If Jim didn't come through for her, she'd just have to cancel the order, a bad business procedure. Either that or try to drive it herself—a most unpleasant prospect, in spite of her bragging to Rees Malory.

She had just hung up after the last abortive telephone call when the door opened and Rees Malory himself stepped inside, his face red from the cold. He was wearing a tan trench coat over his dark suit and carrying a worn leather briefcase.

After his arrival yesterday, he'd presumably disappeared into the maze of the personnel office, and since then she'd been so absorbed in her search for a driver that she'd pushed all thoughts of him from her mind.

She glanced up and gave him a brief, baleful look. The last thing she needed was this interloper to deal with, considering everything else she had on her plate.

He gave her a winning smile, which only escalated her annoyance.

'Good morning,' he said pleasantly.

'Good morning,' she replied grudgingly. 'Did you get yourself all settled with Personnel yesterday?'

'He nodded. 'Yes. I think they're satisfied.'

She scanned the cluttered room for a few seconds. 'I don't know where I'm going to put you.' Then her eye fell on the stenographer's desk across from hers, and she pointed at it. 'You can sit at Sandra's desk for now, I guess,' she said. 'At least until I can find you a desk of your own. Sandra's our secretary, and she's off this week.'

She watched him carefully then to see how he would react. She hadn't really meant it as a put-down, but it would be amusing to see how such a big man would fit himself into Sandra's flimsy chair or deal with the typewriter sitting squarely on top of the desk.

He strolled casually over to it and set the briefcase down on top. Then he looked down at the chair. He rested his hand in his chin, glanced around the room, then without a word he pushed Sandra's chair out of the way, picked up the heavy oak chair that Vanessa reserved for clients against the wall, and carried it back to Sandra's desk.

He shrugged out of his coat and hung it on the rack next to hers, then sat down, settled himself comfortably, and deftly pushed the typewriter out of the way. Then he gazed at her across the space dividing them, a bland look on his face, with more than a hint of amused self-satisfaction in the deep greenish eyes.

OK, Vanessa said to herself, you've won that round, but that's not the only string to my bow. 'Of course,' she said airily to him, 'it may not be necessary to find you a desk.'

He raised a heavy dark eyebrow. 'Oh?' Then he grinned. 'Are you planing to fire me before I've even begun?'

She shrugged. 'Well, how long do you think it will take you?'

'To do what?'

'Whatever you came here to do.'

'Well, since I came here to learn the business, that rather depends on you, doesn't it?'

She narrowed her eyes at him. 'What does that mean?'

'Only that the relevant factor would seem to be your expertise as a teacher.'

She waved a hand angrily in the air. 'Well, you can't learn a business like this overnight, you know! It could take years!'

'Then I guess I'll be here for years,' he said with maddening calm. 'It's quite a pleasant town. I've never been to this part of Oregon, and there's a lot of interesting country to explore.' The corners of his mouth began to twitch again. 'So it looks as though you'd better find that desk for me.'

He turned from her and unsnapped the clips of the briefcase. He peered inside and began examining the contents while she sat there, glaring at him, not sure whether to ignore him or get up and march over to smack the smug grin off his face.

Before she could make up her mind, he glanced up at her. 'Is there something you want me to do right away?'

'No,' was the curt reply. 'I don't have time right now to do any teaching.'

'That's all right,' he said smoothly. 'I'm in no hurry.'

He pulled a manila folder out of his briefcase, set it down, braced his elbows on top of the desk and began to read.

Vanessa reached in the bottom drawer of her desk for the tax forms she had been struggling with, and they both sat there across from each other in a dead silence except for a page being flipped over or a car passing by on the street outside.

As the minutes ticked by, Vanessa would dart him an occasional covert glance, but he never even looked up. What was in the briefcase that was so interesting? And just who was he? What did he want with her, with the business?

She couldn't ask, and there was no way she could find out. The only thing she knew for certain was that he obviously was in no hurry to get his business done and leave. It looked as though she'd be stuck with him for as long as he chose to stay.

At noon he put the file back in his briefcase, stood up and stretched widely. Watching him, Vanessa was struck by the man's undoubted masculine attractions, in spite of her lingering irritation. He had a lean, lithe build, the dark suit hung on him casually but with real elegance, and even his laziest movements seemed purposeful, full of pent-up energy.

'If you're sure there's nothing you want me to do,' he said, moving towards the door, 'I guess I'll go out and get a bite to eat.'

'Yes,' she replied. 'You go ahead.'

'How about you?'

'Oh, I never eat lunch,' she said. 'Maybe just a light snack later in the day.'

'That's not healthy, you know.' He gave her a long, appraising look. 'And you could use a few more pounds.'

Her cheeks reddened, and a sharp retort was on the tip of her tongue. But she checked herself in time. There was no point in starting anything right now. What she wanted was to get him out of here so she could get a look inside that briefcase.

She forced out a smile. 'Now you sound like Harriet,' she said. 'Well, enjoy your lunch.'

When he was gone, she went quickly over to the window to make sure he was safely on his way. There he was, striding off down the ramp and through the parking lot, just as though he owned the place. She ran to the door, turned the lock, then darted over to his desk, on top of which the briefcase was still sitting.

Feeling like a criminal—which, she had to admit, she probably was—but excusing herself on the basis that she was trying to save her company, she bent over and started fumbling with the brass catches at the top. They wouldn't budge. She tried every combination she could think of, but nothing worked.

He'd locked it! She straightened up and stood there
for several seconds, as shivers of foreboding crept up
her spine. Why had he locked it? What could possibly
be inside that he didn't want her to see? What was he
hiding? And worse, obviously hiding it from her! He
must have suspected she'd try to rifle the briefcase the
moment he was gone. A wave of helpless anxiety swept
over her. This was getting serious.

Then it suddenly struck her that she wasn't without
resources, after all. There was a simple way she could
find out whatever she wanted to know about Mr Rees
Malory. She ran back to her desk, snatched up the
telephone and dialled the personnel office. Margaret
Hanson, who had been with the company since her
uncle's day, answered on the first ring.

'Personnel. Miss Hanson speaking.'

'Margaret, this is Vanessa. I need some information on the new man.'

There was a momentary hesitation. 'What new
man?'

'You know. His name is Rees Malory. I sent him
to you yesterday afternoon so you could put him
through the new owner's personnel forms.'

'There must be some mistake, Vanessa,' Margaret
said finally in a bewildered tone. 'I never heard of a
Rees Malory, and he certainly didn't come through
my office yesterday or any other day. What is he, a
new driver?'

Stunned, Vanessa couldn't speak for a moment or
two. 'Never mind,' she said at last. 'I must have been
mistaken.''

She hung up, then stood there for what seemed like hours, plunged in her gloomy thoughts. He'd lied to her! He hadn't gone through Personnel at all. The feeling of helplessness came back in full force. What in the world was she going to do?

CHAPTER TWO

THAT evening during dinner, Vanessa described the day's events to her aunt, expounding heatedly on her suspicions of the menacing Mr Malory. As she should have anticipated, Harriet immediately leapt to his defence.

'But, Vanessa, if he's already an employee of the company, why in the world would he have to fill out all those forms again?' She smiled. 'Do you think he's an imposter?'

'No. Of course not.'

Vanessa bit her lip. Much as she hated to admit it, Harriet was right. He'd been sent by the parent company, was their employee. The memo had said so. Still, she wasn't ready to give in quite yet.

She gave her aunt a stern look. 'Harriet, the man lied to me!'

'Well, dear, did he actually *say* he'd gone through Personnel?'

Vanessa searched her mind. 'Well, I guess he didn't actually say so, but what difference does that make? He certainly led me to believe he had. I *told* him to do it.'

Harriet chuckled. 'Well, just because you tell a man like Rees Malory to do something doesn't mean he will.'

She got up and went to the stove to watch the coffee finish dripping. When it was done, she poured out two cups and brought them back to the table.

'Harriet,' Vanessa was going on earnestly, 'I don't think you realise the seriousness of the situation. It's not funny, and it beats me why you keep making excuses for the man.'

Harriet set the cups down and put an arm around her niece's shoulders. 'Now, Vanessa, calm down. Just ask yourself, what harm can he do? Let's say you're right, that he's been sent here by the company to spy on you. You do a fine job. You have absolutely nothing to fear from him.'

'Oh, it's not that so much,' Vanessa replied glumly. 'I guess what I'm really afraid of is that they plan to take over, to put him—or someone like him—in charge. Harriet, I just couldn't bear that, not after all the hard work I've put into it.'

'Well, now, why would they do that? It's making a nice profit, everything is running smoothly. Besides——'

'Harriet!' she said in a warning tone. 'Don't start.'

'I was only going to mention, dear, that losing control of the business wouldn't really be the end of the world.'

'And do what instead?' Vanessa demanded. Then when Harriet opened her mouth to reply, she held up a hand. 'No, don't tell me. I know what you're going to say. I could find a nice young man, get married, settle down, have babies.'

'There are worse fates, you know,' Harriet said mildly.

'I suppose you mean Robert.'

Harriet's eyes widened. 'Oh, no. Not Robert.'

Vanessa laughed. 'Well, then, who do you have in mind? I haven't noticed any long line of wonderful men on the horizon, beating at my door.'

'Well, dear, if you'd just make a little effort——'

Vanessa drained her coffee and jumped to her feet. 'Goodnight, Harriet,' she announced firmly.

'Where are you going? It's only eight o'clock.'

'I'm going to have a long, hot bath, then go to bed. I'm dead beat. And I still have to find a driver.'

The next morning Vanessa got a late start. Instead of the good night's sleep she had planned on, she'd found herself tossing and turning all night, unable to get thoughts of Rees Malory out of her mind. The few times she'd been able to fall into a troubled slumber, she even dreamt about him! Weird dreams, where he would appear first as the devil incarnate, then as a knight on a white horse.

She'd been in such a hurry that she'd left home without having any breakfast, but as she drove down the main street she had to ask herself why she was rushing. There were no more drivers left on her list to call, no hope of finding anyone to take that consignment to Portland next Thursday. And her stomach was growling.

Instead of parking in her usual spot behind the office, she slid into a space in front of a small restaurant down the street, went inside and ordered an enormous breakfast. When it came, however, she found that all she could choke down was juice, coffee and a piece of dry toast.

There was no point in moving the car, so she walked the half block up the street to her building. Rather than walk clear around to the garage entrance in the back, she went in the front door and through the small public reception room, virtually empty now during the week before Christmas.

From there she went down the corridor to her own office, and when she reached the doorway the first thing she saw was Rees Malory. He was standing at the filing cabinet, his back towards her, going through the contents of the top drawer, totally absorbed. In her rubber-soled boots she hadn't made a sound coming down the hall, so he obviously hadn't heard her coming.

Vanessa stood there for a moment watching him, all her worst suspicions confirmed. There he was, caught in the act. The minute her back was turned he went snooping through her files. She stepped inside the office, folded her arms in front of her and stood there, glaring at his back.

'Just what do you think you're doing?' she demanded in a loud voice.

His hands stilled and for a moment he seemed to freeze. Then, slowly, he swivelled his head around to face her. They stared at each other wordlessly for a few seconds.

'Well?' she said.

He turned around then, and began to walk towards her, a slow smile curling on his mouth, still holding the file he'd been reading. 'Well,' he said evenly, 'since you don't have the time to teach me anything, I thought I'd try to educate myself.' He handed her the file. 'Here, take a look. It's only a standard customer's file. Nothing classified that I can make out.'

Grudgingly she took the file from him and glanced down at it. Her cheeks began to burn. He was right. There was nothing in it that the whole world couldn't see, just a record of shipments they had made for a local company.

'I just wanted to get an idea of how the paperwork was handled,' he explained.

Wordlessly, she handed him back the file and went over to her desk, shrugging off her coat as she went. She didn't know what to say. She even felt a little ashamed of her behaviour. After all, he had been sent here by the parent company to learn the business. She was their employee as much as he was. Why did she have to be so paranoid about it? Couldn't she just follow orders?

She didn't realise that he had come up quietly behind her until she heard his voice. 'Vanessa,' he said softly.

She turned around to see that his face was only inches away from hers. 'Yes? What is it? If you want an apology——'

'I don't want anything,' he said in a low voice. 'Listen, I realise you resent my presence here, and I wish there was some way I could put your mind at ease. I'm not here to spy on you or take over from you. I mean you no harm. I just want to find out more about your operation. Is that so terrible?'

'No,' she muttered, staring down at the floor. 'No, of course not. I'm sorry.' She raised her eyes and gave him a determined look. 'It's just that I didn't want Harriet to sell out in the first place, and ever since she did I've been terrified they'd simply gobble us up.'

He cocked his head to one side and gave her a long look. 'Does the business really mean that much to you?'

'It means everything to me,' she stated firmly.

He shook his head slowly from side to side. 'I think that's rather depressing,' he remarked sadly. 'An attractive young woman like you, capable, intelligent. Is there really nothing else in your life but running this company?'

'That's none of your business,' she snapped. 'I've said I'm sorry. And I'll try to teach you what you want to know. But my personal life is strictly off limits. OK?'

'Sure,' he said with a curt nod. 'I have no problems with that.'

From then on an uneasy truce was established between them. Jim Lake called that weekend to tell her he would probably be able to take the run to Portland for her, that was, if his sniffles and sore throat didn't develop into the flu, and this put her in such a good mood that she could afford to be gracious to Rees Malory.

She still didn't trust him. The episode over the personnel business still rankled. Maybe he hadn't told her an outright lie, but he'd certainly misled her, and she couldn't forget that. But she had to admit Harriet was probably right. What real harm could he do?

She spent the next week teaching him the bare essentials—how to fill out the reams of government forms, going over past union contracts with him, filling him in on standard office procedure, all the basic elements of the trucking business. What she wasn't going to let him examine were her account books, records of profit and loss, or her tax statements. The parent company of course had received that information during the acquisition negotiations, but there was no reason to let him snoop in them.

Then, on the following Friday afternoon, just as they were leaving, he announced that he wouldn't be in the office until after Christmas, which was Wednesday.

'Why not?' she asked, before she could stop herself. What did she care? At least he'd be off her back.

'Oh, I just have a few personal things to take care of.' He gave her a broad grin. 'You've been such a good teacher that I have a fairly good start anyway on how the business is run. And there's so little going on now, right before Christmas, that I don't imagine you'll need me for anything.' He cocked his head to one side and gave her a long look, with just the hint of amusement behind it. 'However, if you really need me, I'll be glad to——'

She held up a hand. 'No. Never mind. I think I'll be able to struggle along without you.'

He had just put on his coat and started towards the door when he turned back to her. 'By the way, have you found a driver yet to take the consignment to Portland?'

She crossed her fingers and held up both hands. 'I think so. Jim Lake called me at home last Sunday and said he'd do it for me if he could. He was coming down with a cold, but if he doesn't have pneumonia by Thursday he'll come through for me. He's very reliable.' She grinned. 'I'm praying for his health.'

'Sounds kind of iffy.'

'Well, yes, but that's part of the territory. In this business you never really know from one minute to the next.'

He smiled. 'You like that, don't you? The uncertainty, the risk, the challenge.'

'I guess so,' she said slowly. 'I never thought of it in quite that way, but you could be right.'

'Yet you're so cautious in your personal life.'

She frowned at him and stuck her chin out. 'What do you know about my personal life?'

'Well, from what I can gather, you don't really have one, that's all.'

She sat down and started pulling on her boots. 'Just because you don't know anything about a subject doesn't mean it doesn't exist,' she muttered.

'No. You're right. Well, have a nice Christmas, Vanessa. Give my regards to Harriet.'

She was just about to ask him what his plans were for the holiday, but in the end decided it would be better not to get on any personal level at all with him. With luck, he'd be gone soon and she'd never see him again.

By then he was gone.

*   *   *

On the following Tuesday evening, Christmas Eve, Vanessa locked up the office at five-thirty and drove through the icy streets to the rambling old house she shared with her aunt on the edge of town.

During the past few days, she'd finished up her Christmas shopping—a cashmere shawl for Harriet, a conservative tie for Robert, a pair of jangly earrings for Sandra—and spent little time in the office herself.

Rees had been right, of course. There was very little to do. And with him and Sandra both gone, it was even a little lonely there all by herself. Funny how in just a little more than a week she'd become used to his presence, even missed him now he was gone.

There had been a light snowfall the night before, rare for southern Oregon, and the Siskiyou Mountains that bordered California rose up before her in a pristine white moonlit glow. It was a beautiful sight, but wreaked havoc with driving conditions.

When she arrived home, she hung up her hat and coat, took off her boots, and padded into the huge living-room where Harriet sat before a blazing fire, stringing popcorn for the tree.

'Oh, there you are,' her aunt said. 'I was getting worried about you. I expected you home hours ago.'

Vanessa went to stand in front of the fire, wriggling her frozen toes and flexing her fingers over the welcome warmth. 'So did I,' she replied. 'I only stuck around because I kept hoping Jim Lake would call to confirm that he's coming Thursday.' She went to the window, pulled aside the curtain and watched the steady snowfall with a sinking heart.

'Well, he said he'd do it, didn't he?'

Vanessa dropped the curtain and came back to the fire. 'Yes, but only if his cold got better. Now, with this snow, he may not even be able to make it over the pass from Medford. Those roads can be tricky this time of year.'

'Oh, dear,' Harriet said abstractedly. 'That's too bad. What will you do if he can't?'

Vanessa rolled her eyes heavenwards and groaned. 'Don't even ask. I haven't a clue.' She didn't dare tell Harriet she was even considering driving it herself. There would be no end of fuss.

Harriet glanced up over her rimless spectacles. 'I presume you've given up on Rees Malory. He *did* say he'd do it.'

Vanessa laughed. 'There was nothing to give up on!' she exclaimed. 'I never expected him to come through in the first place. I told you. It was just smoke.' She came over to sit beside her aunt and scooped up a handful of popcorn. 'I haven't even seen him for the last few days. With luck, he'll just disappear.'

'Well, Jim is very dependable. He'll do it if he can. In the meantime, why don't you try to forget the business for a few days, enjoy the holidays?'

'I think I'll do just that.' She finished up the popcorn, reached for another handful and jumped up. 'I'm going to have a nice hot bath, then I'll help you with the tree.' She stretched widely. 'Thank heavens, a whole day off tomorrow.'

'Is Robert coming for Christmas brunch in the morning?'

'Yes. I told him around eleven o'clock. Is that all right?'

'Fine, dear.' She sighed. 'I wonder what poor Rees Malory is doing for Christmas. Do you think we should have invited him?'

'Oh, Aunt Harriet, you're so incurably sentimental,' Vanessa said with an indulgent smile. 'Rees Malory has probably made tracks back to New York, or wherever he came from, by now. It's a relief, actually, to get rid of him.' She laughed. 'Maybe it was all a bad dream, a nightmare, his showing up like that.'

Harriet gave her a sharp, knowing look. 'It may have been a dream,' she said firmly, 'but I certainly wouldn't call it a nightmare.'

'You're impossible!' With a little wave, Vanessa went out into the hall and ran upstairs to her bedroom.

She had shared the big old house with her aunt since the death of her parents in a car accident when she was only eight years old. Her Uncle Howard had been alive then and, childless themselves, he and Aunt Harriet had accepted her into their home as their own daughter. In fact, except for the photograph on her dresser, she hardly remembered her own parents.

They were pictured there as a happy, ageless young couple, smiling into the camera, and that was how she always thought of them; forever young, almost like contemporaries of her own. Harriet was really the only mother she'd ever known.

After her bath, she dressed in a pair of dark woollen trousers and a bulky white sweater and sat down at the dressing-table to brush out her hair. As she automatically started to pin it up in the usual loose coil at the back of her neck she stopped short, the clasp in her hand, recalling Harriet's comment about her shabby appearance.

She slowly fastened the clasp in place and glanced down at the heavy shapeless sweater that successfully hid every trace of the figure underneath. Did she deliberately go out of her way to be unattractive to men? Was she letting the painful memory of what David had done to her rule her life?

A sudden unbidden vision of Rees Malory jumped into her mind. Actually, although she'd joked to Harriet about the possibility that he had just vanished, she didn't really believe it. It had merely been wishful thinking, whistling in the dark. His unexpected appearance in the office that day, his feeble explanations about the company wanting to 'train' him, just didn't ring true. Robert would be coming over tomorrow, and she could ask him about it then. As Farnham Trucking's lawyer, he'd handled the acquisition and should know the truth of the matter.

She slipped on her glasses and frowned sternly into the mirror, then had to smile at the forbidding image reflected there. It was enough to scare off any man. Good, she thought, jumping to her feet and switching off the light. The last thing she needed was another handsome, seductive man in her life.

It snowed again on Christmas morning. Vanessa awoke late, so exhausted from the busy week at the office and her frantic search for a driver that she'd slept heavily and dreamlessly for a good ten hours. It was past nine now, time to go down and help Harriet.

When she arrived downstairs Harriet was at the kitchen counter, mixing up a batch of blueberry muffins. They had given up the heavy Christmas dinners they used to slave over, and instead served a lavish brunch at eleven o'clock for several friends and neighbours.

'Merry Christmas, Harriet,' she said. She went over and gave her aunt a quick peck on the cheek.

'Merry Christmas, darling. Did you see the fresh snowfall?'

'Yes, it's lovely.' She sniffed the air. 'It smells heavenly in here. What can I do to help?'

'Well, I think I have all the cooking under control, if you'd just set the table and get out the eggnog cups. I think we'll put everything on the sideboard in the dining-room, then people can sit where they like.'

By quarter to eleven, everything seemed to be ready. Vanessa was just giving the dining-room table, gaily decorated with holly and poinsettias, one last glance to see if she'd forgotten anything when the doorbell rang.

'I'll get it,' she called to her aunt.

'It's probably Robert,' Harriet called back. 'He's always the first to arrive.'

Vanessa had been counting on that for her little discussion about Rees Malory. She ran to the door and opened it to a red-faced Robert, all bundled up in heavy outdoor clothing, stamping his feet free of snow.

'Merry Christmas, Robert,' she said, holding the door open wide. 'Come inside before you freeze to death.'

'Merry Christmas, Vanessa,' he said. He stepped inside and closed the door after him. 'Let me just get these things off.'

'Come into the living-room,' she said when he'd hung up his things. 'I want to talk to you before the others get here.'

'Ah, that sounds promising.' He grinned at her, then took her by the hand and leaned over to kiss her lightly on the mouth. 'I hope that means you've decided to marry me after all.'

She laughed. 'Not today, I'm afraid.' She tucked her arm in his and led him into the living-room, where a fire was all laid on the hearth. 'But you can light the fire, if you will, please.'

'That's all I'm good for,' he said with a sigh. He squatted down and lit a match. 'All your menial tasks.' When the fire had caught, he stood up. 'Now, what's the problem?'

'I was wondering what you knew about a man named Rees Malory.'

He thought a minute, then frowned and shook his head. 'Never heard of him. Why?'

'Well, he's been sent here by our new parent company for some reason. He showed up at the office out of the blue, claiming he was sent here to learn the business. According to him, he moves around a lot in the corporate structure, but he was very vague, and somehow nothing he said quite rang true.'

'Why not?'

'Oh, I don't know. He's too smooth, too polished, too confident. I just don't trust him.'

'You make him sound positively sinister. What are you afraid of?'

'I guess what really worries me is that they plan to put him in charge ultimately, that he's here to take over Farnham's. I mean, why else would the company send him here?'

Robert nodded, then thought for a moment. 'Well, all I really did was handle the acquisition,' he said at last. 'I don't actually know for sure what their future plans are, but my impression was that they were perfectly happy with the way you were running it and had no intention of taking over the actual management. My understanding was that their only objective was to diversify their holdings. Maybe your Mr Malory was telling the truth, that he was just sent here to learn more about the business, and when he's through he'll leave.'

'Maybe,' she said dubiously. 'But you hear so many horror stories about these giant corporations, how they take over small companies like ours just to run them at a loss for tax purposes. They're like pirates. Oh, I *wish* Aunt Harriet hadn't sold out!'

'Listen, don't worry about it. I'll look into it for you, but I can't see that there's any question of ruining your business. It's too profitable for that.' He came over and put an arm around her shoulders. 'Now, let's forget it for today, shall we?'

She smiled up at him. 'Yes, of course. Thanks, Robert. You've eased my mind.'

He pulled her more tightly to him. 'I wish you'd let me make that a permanent job,' he said in a low voice.

She looked up at him, wishing for the hundredth time that she could love this good, kind, reliable man. He was so darned *nice*! And she was fond of him. Not only could she depend on him completely, but she knew he'd never break her heart. But, sadly, neither had he ever aroused the least spark in her.

The doorbell chimed loudly, breaking the spell. 'Come on,' she said. 'It sounds as though the others have arrived.'

The next day dawned cold and clear, with a bright sun sparkling on yesterday's snowfall. After breakfast Vanessa got up from the table, where Harriet, still in her robe, was just finishing up a second cup of coffee.

'Well, I guess I'd better be on my way,' she said to her aunt.

Harriet set her cup down with a loud rattle. 'You're not thinking of going in to the office today?' she exclaimed.

Vanessa shrugged. 'Well, I have to, don't I? Jim will be there in an hour and I need to give him the manifest and check out the rig before he heads for Portland.'

'But the roads are a sheet of ice!'

Vanessa laughed. 'Harriet, I've driven on these roads since I was sixteen years old and had my first licence. I'm very careful, and it's only a few miles. Besides, there won't be much traffic the day after Christmas.'

Harriet shook her head sadly. 'I wish you'd pay half as much attention to your personal life as you do to that business.'

'I know you do, dear,' Vanessa replied patiently. 'But let's not go into that now. I have to run.' She started towards the door. 'If all goes well I should be home by noon. See you later.'

In the hall she put on her heavy jacket, boots, scarf and gloves, and went outside. She drew in a deep breath of the bracing, frigid air, then walked the twenty yards or so to the garage, her boots crunching on the cover of ice.

Fortunately, the car started right away, and after it was warmed up she pulled slowly out of the driveway and turned into the street. It was slow going. The sanding trucks hadn't been out yet, and she slipped in several tricky places, but she was a skilful driver, and had been right about the traffic. With virtually no other cars on the streets, she didn't run into any real trouble.

The telephone was ringing when she let herself into the office, and she ran quickly to answer it.

'Farnham Trucking, Vanessa speaking,' she said.

'Hello, Vanessa.' It was a man's voice, faint and croaking on the line. 'This is Jim Lake.'

Her heart sank. 'Yes, Jim?' she said in a tight voice.

'I'm sorry to have to disappoint you about the Portland run, but it looks as though my little cold has turned into a really nasty case of bronchitis. The doc told my wife to keep me in bed or he'd put me in the hospital.' There was a short pause, then a sneeze, then a paroxysm of coughing. 'I would have called you sooner, but I kept hoping I'd get better.'

He sounded terrible, and was obviously really sick. 'I'm sorry, too, Jim,' she said with a sigh. 'You'd better stay in bed and take care of yourself.'

'What'll you do about the run?'

'Don't worry about that. I'll try to find another driver, but I can always take it myself if I have to.'

'Reports are that the road is pretty bad up north.'

'Well, we'll see. If we can't deliver, we can't deliver. I'd better get busy now, Jim. I'll talk to you later. Get well soon.'

After they hung up Vanessa put her head in her hands and groaned aloud. Although she was confident of her driving, she didn't look forward to a three-hour haul on these icy roads. Actually, a heavy truck had less control than a smaller vehicle. Once it started slipping there was practically no hope of regaining control.

In normal circumstances, she would have called the consignee in Portland and told them it wasn't possible to deliver today in the poor road conditions. It was a large order, and they were one of her best customers. She hated to disappoint them, but they would have understood. No one could expect the impossible, and it sometimes happened in the winter that certain deliveries simply couldn't be made.

But the advent of Rees Malory, who for all she knew was a spy sent to uncover evidence of her poor management, made it imperative to come through for them. She'd just have to do it herself and hope for the best. Maybe by the time she got going the sanding crews would have made the roads more passable.

Just then there came from outside the sound of a car door slamming, heavy footsteps coming closer. She looked up, startled. Who in the world would be showing up now? Then the door opened, and Rees Malory stepped inside. He was wearing a thick tartan woollen jacket, heavy boots and leather gloves.

He smiled at her. 'Good morning, boss,' he said. 'Is the truck all loaded and ready to go?'

CHAPTER THREE

VANESSA had been so certain he wouldn't show up that for a moment all she could do was stare at him, speechless. Finally she found her voice.

'What are you doing here?'

His dark eyebrows knitted together in a puzzled frown. 'You said you needed someone to drive today. It *is* the day after Christmas, isn't it?'

'Well, yes,' she faltered. 'But I'm just so surprised to see you here. I mean, I guess I didn't really expect you to go through with it.'

'I don't see why not. I told you I would, didn't I?'

She nodded. 'Yes. You did.'

'Well, then, let's get the show on the road. Is the rig loaded?'

She gave herself a little shake. 'Yes, it is. But what about a trucker's driving licence? I can't let you go without that.'

He reached in his pocket, pulled out a flat leather wallet and flipped it open. 'I've taken care of that. Would you care to inspect it?'

She gave it a cursory glance, just enough to see that he had dark brown hair, blue-green eyes, was six feet two inches tall and weighed one hundred and eighty pounds, all of which she could have guessed. It also gave his birthdate. Calculating swiftly, she came up with the fact that he was thirty-six years old. As she read, a slow anger began to boil up in her.

She gave him a dirty look. 'Why didn't you tell me? You could have saved me a lot of grief.'

'Well, I wasn't sure I could get the licence in time and didn't want to get your hopes up in case it didn't work out.'

She eyed him suspiciously. 'Just how did you get a trucker's licence so fast? It usually takes weeks, sometimes months. You did it in days.'

He shrugged. 'Oh, I just gave them a hard luck story.'

She didn't believe him, and was about to tell him so when he crossed the room to stand before her, not a foot away, hands on hips, his face like stone.

'Listen, do you want me to go or not?'

'Well, yes,' she faltered. 'Of course I do.'

'Then what do you care how I got that licence so fast? Let's get the show on the road.'

'All right, then,' she said, handing it back to him. 'It looks to be in order. I'll get the manifest for you and give you directions where to go.' Still a little dazed, she went over to the filing cabinet against the wall, pulled out the Portland file, then came back and handed it to him. 'Are you sure you want to do this?' she asked, looking up at him with a worried frown. 'The roads are in pretty bad shape, and you're not used to the truck you'll be driving. It could be dangerous.'

Their eyes met, and before she realised what his intention was he had placed the palm of one hand lightly on her cheek. 'Don't worry about it, boss,' he said softly. 'I'll get your shipment delivered for you.'

She gazed up at him, locked in those deep green eyes, unable to say a word. The touch of his hand, cool and gentle on her face, his tone of voice, the way he was looking at her, was all so pleasant that she never wanted it to end. An insidious warmth began to steal over her, and for a moment she forgot that this man was the enemy.

In the next moment she came to her senses. She turned her head away. 'Well, just be careful,' she said.

The hand dropped from her face as though it had been burned, and he stepped back a pace from her. 'Oh, I'm a very cautious type,' he said. 'I never allow myself to get caught in a situation I'm not confident I can easily get out of.'

I'll just bet you don't, she said grimly to herself. 'Well, if you think you can handle it ...'

He shrugged. 'I can only give it a try. If I think I can't make it, I'll say so.' He took the file from her and turned to go.

Then a sudden suspicion struck her. 'Just a minute,' she called to him. When he turned around she walked slowly over to him and gave him a long, careful look. 'There's one thing I'm rather curious about,' she said in a tight voice. 'If you're so familiar with trucks that you're able to get a licence this fast, why do you need me to teach you the business?'

For one fleeting moment he looked definitely nonplussed. He dropped his eyes and the confident smile faded. It didn't last long, however, and in the next instant he was smiling with the usual self-assurance she had come to expect from him.

He waved a hand in the air. 'Just because I'm ignorant about the trucking business doesn't mean I don't know how to drive. And in some of my other jobs I've had to handle trucks. Listen,' he said in a terse voice. 'Do you want me to do this or not?'

'Yes, of course I do,' she replied quickly. 'In fact, you've saved my life.' At this point she couldn't afford to get his dander up. What would she do if he left her high and dry without a driver? 'I'm sorry,' she said, forcing out a penitent smile. 'I'm afraid I just have a naturally suspicious nature.'

He crossed his arms in front of him and narrowed his eyes at her. 'All right, then, you tell me something. What would you have done if I hadn't shown up?'

She gave him a startled look. Was this some kind of test? 'Well, I did have a driver lined up, but he conked out on me at the last minute.' She raised her chin. 'As a last resort, however, I would have done it myself.'

His eyes flew open. 'You really meant it?' She nodded. 'Well, I'll be darned,' he said. He rubbed his chin thoughtfully. 'You know, you're an amazing girl.' He cocked his head to one side. 'And a damned attractive one, too, if you'd only make a little effort.'

She gave him a withering look, then marched past him to the door and opened it, letting in a blast of frigid air. 'Come on,' she called. 'I'll check you out on the rig.'

*   *   *

That day seemed endless. She stayed in the office until noon, jumping every time the telephone rang, knowing he couldn't possibly have made it to Portland yet, even in perfect weather, and dreading a call from the state highway patrol informing her that the truck had crashed or slid off the highway.

She had visions of the carefully packed cargo spilled and scattered all over the icy road, the rig on its side, smashed, perhaps on fire, the driver's body trapped inside or thrown from the cab and lying broken and bleeding beside it. She must have been out of her mind to let Rees take the run. Even the most experienced driver would have trouble in these conditions.

At eleven o'clock it started snowing again, fine powdery flakes that clung tenaciously to the still-frozen streets, and she finally decided there was no point getting stuck in the office, snow-bound. She could just as well do her fretting at home. It was time to get the month-end billings prepared anyway, and she could work on that at the house as well.

She was just about to leave when the telephone rang shrilly in the empty office. A cold chill gripped her heart, a certainty that it would be the highway patrol, calling to tell her of a terrible accident . . .

She snatched it up. 'Yes?'

There was a short silence, then a woman's voice came on the line. 'Is this the Farnham Trucking Company?'

'Yes, it is,' she replied in a tight voice.

'I wonder if I might speak to Rees Malory, please?'

Vanessa closed her eyes, leaned back in her chair and expelled a long breath of sheer relief. 'I'm sorry,' she said at last. 'He isn't here right now. Can I take a message?'

'Yes, please. Would you tell him that Susan called and would like to speak to him?'

'Susan,' she repeated dully. 'Is that all?'

'Yes. He'll know the number. Thanks a lot. Goodbye.'

The telephone went dead as the connection was broken, and Vanessa slowly hung up the receiver. Susan, she thought. Who in the world could Susan be? It was the first call he'd received since he'd been there.

Well, it was none of her business. It stood to reason that a man like Rees Malory would have a woman tucked away somewhere. She scribbled the message on a piece of paper and threw it on the top of Sandra's desk, where he would be sure to see it when he got back—*if* he got back.

She spent the rest of the day at home, making one futile attempt after another to distract herself, working on the books, reading, making a batch of fudge, even, when all else failed, sitting in the den with Harriet and watching the talk shows. Nothing seemed to work, however, and she ended up pacing around the room and wringing her hands, until finally Harriet blew.

'For heaven's sake, child!' she called to her in exasperation. 'Will you either settle down or get out of here and leave me in peace! This is my favourite programme.'

Vanessa gave the television set a look of utter contempt. 'I don't see how you can watch that garbage.'

'Well, it's better than prowling around fretting about Rees Malory.'

'I'm not fretting about him,' she retorted. 'It's the truck, the consignment, I'm worried about. I should never have agreed to let him take it.'

'Well, why did you then?' Harriet asked mildly.

'I was desperate, that's why! Besides, when he showed up this morning all ready to go, he just seemed to take over. The next thing I knew he was driving off.'

Harriet chuckled. 'I can see how he'd do that. He's that kind of man.'

Vanessa stamped her foot angrily. 'Oh, you're impossible!' she cried, and stalked out of the room.

By five o'clock that afternoon she'd given up hope. She stood at the living-room window, gazing dejectedly out at the white blanket that covered everything in sight. It was already dark outside, but it had stopped snowing, and the dark winter sky was filled with bright twinkling stars.

Just then the telephone rang. She ran into the hall and snatched up the receiver. 'Yes?'

'Hi, Vanessa. It's me.'

'Oh, hello, Robert,' she said dully.

'Please,' he said in a joking tone. 'Try to restrain your enthusiasm.'

'I'm sorry, Robert. It's just that I sent a truck out this morning and haven't heard from the driver yet.'

'Well, the roads are no picnic, let me tell you. What fell today is now frozen over. Listen, I just called to tell you I have to go out of town on a case and will be gone at least two weeks.'

'Well, I'll miss you, Robert,' she replied distractedly, anxious to hang up and free the line.

'I hope you mean that.' There was a short silence. 'Anyway,' he went on, 'the main reason I'm calling is to tell you that now I'm afraid I won't have time to look into your mystery man for you. If it's really important I can have someone else in the office do it.'

'No,' she said hurriedly. 'I'd rather no one else knew about my concern. Besides, I think I might have been jumping the gun with my suspicions. So let's just forget about it until you come back. By then I should have a clearer picture of what's really going on.'

'Well, if you're sure.'

'I'm sure. Don't worry about it. He's probably just what he says he is, and I was foolish to draw the wrong conclusions.'

'Well, goodbye, then,' he said hesitantly. 'I'll call you when I get back.'

'Right. Goodbye. And good luck with your case.'

Just as she replaced the receiver the telephone jangled in her hand and she picked it up immediately. 'Hello.'

'Hi, boss,' came Rees Malory's deep masculine voice. 'Just checking in with you.'

'Rees!' she blurted without thinking. Almost overcome with relief, she sank weakly down on the chair beside the table. 'Where are you?'

'In Portland. Where else?'

'Then you made it all right.'

'Sure.' He laughed. 'Although I'll have to admit there were moments when I had my doubts.'

Now that her fears were allayed, a slow anger began to simmer inside her. 'Well, you could have called me sooner!' she said. 'I've been half out of my mind with worry all day.'

'About me? I'm flattered.'

'No, not about you,' she retorted stonily. 'About the shipment. Is it OK?'

'In tiptop shape. In fact,' he added drily, 'that's why I didn't call earlier. I had to unload the whole kit and caboodle myself. Apparently they're no more anxious to work the day after Christmas in Portland than they are anywhere else.'

She had to laugh. 'Oh, well, a big strong man like you shouldn't complain about a little thing like that.'

'Oh? And what would you have done if you'd driven yourself?'

'*Touché*,' she agreed. 'You have a good point. I probably would have sat there until someone took pity on me and came to my rescue.'

'Ah, a damsel in distress underneath all that confidence and authority. I like that.' He paused for a moment, but when she didn't say anything, went on. 'Anyway, I just wanted to let you know I made your delivery all right. However, I don't think I'll try to drive back tonight.'

'No, of course not. I wouldn't expect you to. What about the truck?'

'It's safely tucked away at the customer's warehouse. I'll pick it up in the morning and head back. In the meantime, the first item on my agenda is a stiff drink, then an enormous steak dinner.'

'Where will you stay?' she asked, then added quickly, 'In case I need to get hold of you.'

He gave her a number. 'If I'm not around, you can leave a message.'

It was on the tip of her tongue to ask him if he was at a hotel or had found more personal accommodation, but she bit back the question. It was none of her business.

'Well, I'll say goodbye now,' he said. 'I'll probably see you some time tomorrow.'

'Right. Goodbye, then. And Rees?'

'Yes?'

'Thanks a lot for coming through for me.'

'Any time, boss. Any time.'

He broke the connection then, and Vanessa sat there for several moments with the dead receiver in her hand, filled with a strange warm glow of satisfaction, yet still piqued about Rees's plans for the evening. Suddenly she realised that Harriet was standing in the doorway, watching her.

'Well, I must say,' her aunt commented as she walked towards her, 'you look like the cat that's swallowed the canary. I take it that was Rees on the line, telling you he arrived safe and sound.'

It dawned on Vanessa then that not only was she still holding the telephone in her hand, but that her mouth was set in a decidedly foolish grin. She slammed down the receiver and jumped to her feet.

'Yes. Truck and shipment are both in fine shape.'

'Not to mention the driver.'

'Yes, Aunt Harriet,' she agreed with a sigh, too relieved to argue about semantics. 'The driver, too.'

* * *

The next day at lunch, Vanessa announced that she was going into the office for a while that afternoon. The bitter cold front had passed over during the night, turning the snow to rain, the icy streets to a dirty grey slush, and making driving conditions far less hazardous.

'Why on earth do you want to do that?' Harriet asked. 'Now that your Portland problem has been solved there really isn't much going on so soon after Christmas. No one else will be there.'

'I know,' Vanessa replied, getting up from the table. 'But it'll be quiet, and there are several things I've been putting off for too long. Sandra is so afraid of driving in the snow that she hasn't been in all week, and the filing has reached epidemic proportions by now. Not,' she added wryly, 'that I count much on her help. Efficiency isn't her strong point, I'm afraid.'

Harriet chuckled. 'Well, I warned you about her. Her mother was the same way, just filling in time until she got married. Sensible girl, I always thought.' She got up and started clearing the table. 'I was hoping you'd go with me today to visit Mrs Perkins. You know she's in the hospital again with another back surgery. Surely Sandra can at least catch up on the filing when she shows up on Monday.'

'No, thanks, Harriet!' Vanessa said with feeling. Her aunt's sickly friends were legion and always seemed to be recuperating from something. 'It's not just the filing. I still have the month-end billings to do, and I've got to finish calculating our next income tax instalment. It's due in January.'

'Well, all right. If you really feel you must.'

Vanessa hesitated at the door. As she watched her aunt, busy now at the sink rinsing off the lunch dishes, she was hit by a sudden feeling of guilt. It wouldn't hurt her to go with her to visit her friend. The work she planned to do wasn't that pressing, and most of it *was* Sandra's responsibility.

'Harriet,' she said. 'If you were really counting on me to go with you, I guess the income tax can wait. Lord knows I've put it off this long; another few days won't hurt.'

Harriet turned around and smiled at her. 'No. You go ahead. I know how important the business is to you. You've done such a fine job since Howard died that I shouldn't interfere.'

'Are you sure?' Such a sudden change of heart was rare, coming from her aunt, who usually hung on tenaciously until she got what she wanted from her.

Harriet nodded. 'Positive.' She started running water into the dish pan. 'Besides,' she called over her shoulder, 'I wouldn't want you to miss Rees Malory when he comes back from Portland.' She turned around and gave her niece a complacent look. 'That *is* the main reason you want to go to the office today, isn't it?'

'Of course not! What ever gave you such an idea?'

'Oh, sorry,' Harriet murmured. 'My mistake.'

Vanessa stood there, fuming inwardly for a moment or two and trying to come up with an appropriate retort. Yet she knew it was hopeless. Once Harriet got an idea in her head, especially if it pertained to a potential romance, she was like a dog with a bone. The best thing would be to ignore it. As she stalked out of the room, however, she was positive she could hear a low chuckle of satisfaction emanating from the kitchen sink.

The office was cold and dreary when she arrived. She turned on the heat and a few lights, then settled down behind her desk to tackle the hated tax forms. Robert usually helped her with them but, since he wasn't available at the moment, she felt she had to at least make the attempt to figure them out herself.

Try as she might to concentrate, however, her mind kept wandering, her ears perked up at every noise coming from the yard outside. Finally she threw down her pencil, leaned her elbows on the top of the desk and put her chin in her hands, staring into space.

Could Harriet be right? Was it true that the real reason she wanted to come into the office today was to be there when Rees got back? Odd how he'd changed overnight in her mind from a distant enemy named Malory to a lifesaver called Rees. Well, he had bailed her out of a sticky situation. It was only natural to be grateful.

Besides, since it looked as though she was stuck with him for a while whether she liked it or not, she might as well bow gracefully to the inevitable. He had his orders and she had hers. She was to teach him the business, and that's what she'd better do.

In that case, he'd need a desk and chair. She got up and walked down the hall to the storage room where all the old equipment was kept to see if she could find something suitable. The room was dim and dusty and full of discarded chairs with broken springs, wobbly tables with legs missing, a filing cabinet whose drawers no longer worked, several cartons of old records, a broken typewriter.

Finally she came across an old desk Howard used to use. It was badly scarred and the bottom drawer was stuck tight, but it would do for the short time Rees would be there. She'd need help moving it, however. It would have to wait until Monday, when the men came.

Just then she heard the office door open and shut, and she jumped as a sudden shock of warmth hit her. He was back! She half ran down the hall to the office, a glad smile of welcome on her lips.

But it wasn't Rees. Standing there forlornly in the middle of the room was a small blonde girl, all bundled up against the weather and smiling anxiously.

Vanessa's face fell. 'Sandra!' she said. 'What on earth are you doing here?'

'Well, I know I'm late, and I'm sorry I missed work all week,' the girl said in a rush. 'But I just can't drive in that awful snow. I knew you'd be mad, so today when it started to melt I thought I'd try to get in.'

Her lower lip was trembling, her blue eyes wide with anxiety, and Vanessa could see that the girl was on the verge of tears. She felt like some kind of monster.

'Oh, come on, Sandra,' she said cheerfully. 'Stop that. I never expected you to come in and you might as well have stayed home today.' The inspiration hit her. 'But as long as you're here, you can help me move some furniture in here from the store-room. It's for the new man.'

'Sure, Vanessa,' the girl said, brightening. She wiped her eyes with the back of her hand. 'What new man?'

'Oh, the company sent in a man they want me to teach the business to, and he needs a desk and chair. I think between us we can manage.'

They went back to the store-room, where Vanessa pointed out the things she wanted moved. 'Here,' she said, moving to the far edge of the huge desk. 'I'll push and you pull.'

She put all her weight behind it, tensing the muscles in her legs and arms to breaking-point, but the old monster wouldn't budge. With each passing moment, she grew more and more frustrated. It seemed incredible that two strong young women couldn't manage to move one desk even a few inches.

Finally, panting and perspiring, she gave it up. 'I'll have to wait and get some of the men to move it on Monday.'

Suddenly there came a voice from the direction of the office. 'Hey! Anybody here?' Then the sound of footsteps coming towards the store-room, and in the next moment Rees Malory appeared in the doorway, grinning at the two women. 'What's going on? Were you planning to move away while I was gone?'

'You're back,' Vanessa stammered, knowing it sounded stupid, but horribly embarrassed to be caught trying to move the desk for his sake, most of all because she'd failed.

'Who's your friend?' he asked, with a glance at Sandra.

Vanessa looked over at the girl, who was standing there with her mouth open, staring at Rees as though the sun had just risen in the east. 'This is Sandra Elliot, my office help. Rees Malory.'

Rees stepped over to Sandra, reached for her hand and shook it solemnly. 'I'm very pleased to meet you, Sandra.'

Sandra immediately started to giggle. Vanessa could have slapped her. The last thing this man needed was another adoring female. Then she checked herself. *Another* adoring female? What put that stupid idea in her head?

'Well, now that you're here,' she said briskly, 'you can help us move this desk into the office.'

He went over to the desk and stood there, looking down at it thoughtfully for several seconds, chin in hand. Then he stooped down to inspect the underside, reaching in a hand and jiggling something that sounded metallic. He stood up, brushing off his hands.

'The casters were locked,' he said. 'No wonder you couldn't move it. Here, I'll push it if you two ladies will guide it in the right direction. It should glide along smoothly now.'

'Well,' Vanessa said, leaning over and grabbing hold of it, 'I'm glad to see it didn't take brawn after all.'

He caught her eye and smiled at her over the desk. 'No,' he said mildly. 'Just brains.'

She was about to make a stinging retort, but she bit it back just in time, forced to see the humour of the situation. Here they'd been, struggling with the recalcitrant monster, when all along it would have been a simple matter to move it by themselves if only they'd

known about the locked casters. Besides, he seemed
to be smiling *with* her, not at her.

'OK,' she said, returning the smile. 'I'll have to give
you that one. Come on, Sandra, let's get to work.'

From then on, the three of them settled into a smooth
daily working routine, amicable enough on the
surface, although Vanessa still cringed every time
Sandra gave Rees another of those adoring looks or
offered to get his coffee or type up one of his reports.

To her relief, Harriet seemed to have lost interest
in him, until one night a few weeks later at the dinner
table.

'Tell me,' she said, 'how are things working out
with Rees Malory by now?'

Vanessa gave her aunt a suspicious look. 'All right,'
she said tentatively.

'The poor man must be lonely here in a strange
town, with no friends or family. I think it would be
nice to invite him over to dinner one night.'

Vanessa almost choked on her roast beef. 'No!' she
said in a strangled voice when she'd finished coughing.
'Don't you dare. Besides,' she added drily, 'I doubt
very much that Rees Malory has ever been lonely in
his life.'

'Oh, come now, Vanessa, surely you're not still
upset that he was sent here? It's not his fault, after
all. Are you still worried that he's a spy?'

'No,' Vanessa said slowly. 'It's not that. In fact, as
it's turned out, he really doesn't know anything about

the business, but he's quick to catch on. Best of all, he doesn't get in my way.'

'Well, I'm glad to hear it. And you don't think he was sent here to take over, as you did at first?'

'Well, if he was, he hides it well. He never countermands any of my orders or argues with my decisions. In fact, much as I hate to admit it, he's actually come to be a help to me in the dispatch office. He obviously has an accounting background, and if it wasn't that I don't want him to know too much about our financial situation I would gladly have given him the January tax statement to do.'

'Well, then, why not try to be more hospitable?'

'For one thing, I'm against mixing business and socialising, just as a matter of policy. For another, I doubt if he'd come. He disappears every weekend and, unless I miss my guess, he has a pretty active social life somewhere else.'

Harriet widened innocent grey eyes. 'Well, it can't hurt to ask.'

'Just don't. Please, Harriet. Don't do it. I forbid it.'

That night, having delayed as long as she decently could, Vanessa finally plunged into the January tax forms herself. The statement was due soon and, with Robert unavailable to help her, she had no choice but to try to decipher the instructions and penetrate the mysteries of capital gains and depreciation on her own.

She started working on it right after dinner. By midnight, her eyes bleary, the pages of figures swimming before her, she finished it at last. Tomorrow she'd give it to Sandra to type up.

The next day, while Sandra was poring over the forms she'd pencilled in, Vanessa took Rees out to the loading shed to introduce him to Jim Lake, the trucker from Medford who drove for her occasionally.

'Jim is one of my most dependable drivers,' she explained as they went inside the shed. 'I only wish I could get him on a permanent basis.'

'Why can't you?'

'Oh, he likes being independent,' she explained. 'And he won't join the union. Of course, that doesn't make him very popular with the other drivers, so I only use him when I don't have anyone else to send.'

'Do you have much union trouble, then?' he asked.

'No, but that's because we usually give them pretty much what they ask for.'

'How often do you negotiate?'

'Our contracts with them usually run for four years. In fact, we're due to sign a new one this year.' She looked up to see Jim, coming towards them. 'Here's Jim now.'

She introduced them and, while the two men chatted easily about the inner workings of the truck Jim was going to take out that day, she found herself mentally comparing them. Jim was a typical burly trucker, roughly dressed in worn jeans, heavy tartan shirt and boots, while Rees, as always, looked as though he'd just stepped out of a band-box, his clothes immaculate, his grooming impeccable. Yet just a few weeks ago he'd seemed just as much at ease in the same kind of outfit Jim had on now.

She still knew virtually nothing about Rees's private life. He showed up at work on time and left when she did but, aside from the fact that she knew he was staying at a local hotel, what he did in his spare time and what his past life had been were still a total mystery to her.

Rees and Jim were out in the yard now. Jim had climbed into the cab of the truck, whose motor was warming up, and she went out to join them. She handed Jim the manifest, then she and Rees stood there, watching as he drove off.

They had just started walking back to the office when a car pulled up into the yard, and a second later Harriet got out.

'Hello,' she said, walking towards them. 'I had to come into town today to do some shopping and thought I'd drop by for a minute.' She turned to Rees. 'How are you, Rees? I hope your training is going smoothly.'

'Perfectly,' he said with a smile. He nodded at Vanessa. 'Your niece is an excellent teacher.'

'Well, good,' Harriet beamed. 'I'm happy it's all working out so well. I'm afraid I haven't even seen you since the day you got here. Terribly remiss of me. I'm not usually so inhospitable to newcomers in town.'

She hesitated for a moment, one finger on her lips, then her eyes lit up, as though she'd just been struck by a brilliant idea. It was then that Vanessa had her first horrified inkling of what her aunt was up to. But before she could even think of a way to stop her,

Harriet had put a hand on Rees's arm and was looking up into his face with a bright smile.

'I'll tell you what. Why don't you come over for dinner this weekend? Shall we say Saturday night?'

CHAPTER FOUR

REES hesitated, obviously taken aback by the sudden invitation, while Vanessa only stood there, writhing in an agony of embarrassment at the spot Harriet had put them both in. She glared at her aunt, trying to signal her with her eyes to back off, but when Harriet firmly refused to acknowledge her dirty looks she knew she had to intervene.

'Oh, Harriet,' she said in a rush, 'I'm sure Rees has better things to do with his weekends than a dull dinner at our house.'

He shot her a swift, inscrutable glance. 'Not at all,' he said. He turned his gaze on Harriet. 'But I'm afraid Saturday night is out. I already have other plans.'

Vanessa breathed a sigh of relief. But she discovered that she was rejoicing prematurely when Harriet, still studiously avoiding her glance, pressed on, undaunted.

'Well, then, how about Sunday?'

'Yes,' he said, with no hesitation. 'Sunday would be fine.'

'Good. We'll expect you around seven o'clock.' When she did look at Vanessa, it was to give her a triumphant grin, still managing to ignore the black look directed her way. 'Well, I'd better be off now. I still have my errands to run, and I know you two are very busy.'

Vanessa, still rigid with anger, stood there watching until her aunt's car disappeared from view. She didn't dare even look at Rees, who she had no doubt was enjoying the whole thing immensely. She turned on her heel and, with eyes firmly fixed straight in front of her, began to march back to the office. She could hear his footsteps on the pavement behind her, following her, and quickened her pace.

But she wasn't quite fast enough. At the door, he touched her lightly on the arm. 'Vanessa,' he said.

The touch of his hand went through her like an electric shock. This is a very dangerous man, she warned herself, and she mentally gathered all her forces of resistance against him.

'What?' she said curtly.

The pressure on her arm increased slightly. 'Would you please turn around?' he asked mildly. 'I can't talk to the back of your head.'

Slowly she turned and looked up at him. A breeze had come up, ruffling his dark hair, and the pale January sun gleaming on his dark hair brought out the golden highlights. The glint of amusement in his eyes, a cool deep green today, and the hint of a smile on the thin, chiselled lips were exactly as she had anticipated, and only made her feel more trapped.

She shook his hand off her arm. 'What is it, Rees? I have work to do.'

'Listen, don't think I didn't realise that the last thing you wanted was for me to accept your aunt's dinner invitation. I'm not stupid, you know.' He laughed. 'Lord, if looks could kill, poor Harriet would have been carried out of here in a hearse.'

Vanessa put her hands on her hips and glared at him. 'Well, then, if you're so smart, why did you accept? A clever man like you could have wriggled out of it somehow.'

He shrugged. 'Simple courtesy. If she's kind enough to take pity on a poor lonely stranger in town, wouldn't it be rather boorish of me to refuse?'

The expression on his face was innocent enough, his tone quite serious, but of course he was still laughing at her, and she knew that if she once let this man get the upper hand over her she'd be lost.

'Well,' she said sweetly, 'I hope you and Harriet enjoy your dinner. I happen to have other plans.' She turned and opened the office door.

Before she could get inside, however, he'd moved swiftly and stretched out a hand to bar her way. 'Oh, come on, Vanessa, lighten up. How can one dinner hurt you?' He spread his arms wide and grinned. 'What have you got against me? I'm harmless.'

With great dignity, she pulled herself up to her full five five feet seven. 'I have nothing against you,' she said with elaborate patience. 'I merely have another engagement Sunday.'

'I don't believe you,' he stated flatly.

She was about to argue, to continue the charade, but something told her he'd persist until he'd finally broken her down. She might as well be honest with him and tell him the truth. The only problem was that she wasn't quite certain herself by now what the real truth of the matter was.

She decided to temporise. 'All right, then. I just don't believe in mixing my business and social lives.

We have to work together. I've accepted that. I admit I resented it at first, but it seems to be working out all right. I'm even grateful for your help. But that's where it ends. At the office.'

He gave her a long look, an appraising look, as though he could penetrate to the very core of her true feelings. 'You know,' he said at last, 'I think you're making an awful lot out of nothing. You act as though a simple dinner between business associates would necessarily lead to a flaming love affair or a lifetime commitment or something. Believe me, I have no such plans.'

Vanessa's face went up in flame. She began to sputter out a garbled reply, when he held up a hand to stop her.

'I'm not through. Now, while I admit you could be a very attractive young woman if you made the least effort, I don't believe in mixing personal relations with business either. Besides, I won't be around much longer to bother you.'

'Good!' she finally managed to blurt out. 'That's just fine by me.'

He nodded. 'All right, then, so long as we understand each other, what in the world do you stand to lose by sitting down at the table through one meal with me? Or to gain by offending your aunt?'

Vanessa stared stonily down at the ground. He was right, of course. She'd been behaving like a child. Although it galled her to come out second best in the little contretemps, she did have sense enough to know when she was beaten. She might as well concede and make as graceful a retreat as possible.

She finally managed a smile. 'You do have a point,' she said with a sigh. 'I'm sorry.'

He nodded with satisfaction. 'Good.' Then he tilted his head to one side and gave her a quirky smile. 'Does that mean you'll break your other date for Sunday?'

She narrowed her eyes at him. 'Don't push your luck, Mister,' she snapped, and pushed past him into the office, head held high, shoulders squared.

She could hear his laughter, following her all the way inside. '*Damn* the man!' she muttered, as she settled herself behind her desk. He'd beaten her at her own game once again.

In the days that followed, Vanessa found herself mulling over that last conversation again and again. It would crop up in the oddest places: in the middle of a business meeting with the union representative, over a meal with Harriet, helping Sandra decipher her scribbled figures on the tax forms she was typing.

She had to admit that he'd handled the whole thing adroitly, with a practised confidence and charm that revealed his expertise at one-upmanship beautifully. She'd certainly come out second best, and she still wasn't quite sure how he'd done it. She'd ended not only by agreeing to show up at the dinner on Sunday night, but by feeling like a perfect fool for the fuss she'd put up about it.

Nor could she quite erase the memory of her re-action to the touch of his hand on her arm. She had been so sure of herself and her determination not to get involved with him, and yet his resolve to do exactly the same thing seemed to be at least as determined as her own. And no matter how many times she told herself that his opinion of her didn't matter in the slightest, the fact that he didn't find her attractive stuck in her craw like a lump of lead.

At odd moments, she would catch herself staring at him across the room in the office, bedevilled by a host of unanswered questions. Why hadn't he been able to make it on Saturday? Where did he go at weekends? Was he seriously involved with a woman? The mysterious Susan, perhaps? What was his background? Where would he go when he left here?

Her imagination ran riot. She pictured a steady procession of beautiful, sophisticated women in his life, past, present and future, of wild orgies with glamorous chorus girls, weekend trysts with a host of adoring females, each vision more lurid and fanciful than the last. Occasionally he would look up suddenly from whatever he was doing and catch her, and no matter how quickly she dropped her eyes she knew he'd seen, and knew too from the way her cheeks burned that he was well aware of her chagrin.

She was alone in the office early next morning, going through the current stack of mail. Most of it turned out to be junk: year-end advertisements, catalogues, a few bills, some belated Christmas cards.

There was one letter from the new parent company, a thick creamy envelope with the return address in fine script—Global Enterprises in New York—and she automatically started to open it, until she saw, just in time, that it was addressed not to her but to Rees Malory.

She held the envelope in her hand and stared down at it. Why was the head office writing to him? Well, he was an employee, wasn't he? Why shouldn't they communicate with him? Still, curiosity burned within her. She was alone in the office. Should she or shouldn't she?

Quickly, she went over to the window and held the envelope up against the sunshine pouring through. She could see faint lines of typing, but even in the strongest light there was no way she could make out the words. The paper was too thick. For one fleeting moment she was tempted to steam it open, but before the idea could seriously take hold in her mind she turned around and tossed the letter on top of his desk, putting temptation firmly behind her, ashamed of herself for even considering such a thing.

When Rees appeared, a few minutes later, she watched him carefully to see what he'd do. The top of his desk was bare except for that letter. There was no way he could miss it. After hanging up his coat, he stood at his desk for a moment, gazing down at the envelope. Then, without a word, he picked it up and slipped it in the inside pocket of his suit jacket.

He wasn't even going to open it in front of her! He must have something to hide. The normal thing would have been for him to open it right there, make some comment about its contents. Instead he was being secretive about it, and all her old fears about the reason for his presence there rose up within her once again, just when she was beginning to trust him.

*   *   *

That Friday afternoon they closed up the office at five o'clock, as usual, and walked together out to the yard, where his dark rental Peugeot was parked next to her small Toyota. She hesitated before getting inside, wondering if she should mention seeing him on Sunday, but decided not to when she saw he was already in the Peugeot and firing up the engine.

She started her own car and was just backing out of her parking space when she noticed that he was leaning out of the open door and calling to her. She rolled her window down.

'I'm sorry,' she said. 'I didn't hear you.'

'I just said I'll see you Sunday night.'

'Yes,' she replied, nodding briefly.

It was on the tip of her tongue to ask him where he was off to over the weekend, but just then his door slammed shut, he shot out past her and, with a wave, moved down the driveway to the street.

She sat there for several moments, the engine idling, and the sudden thought came to her that, in spite of all her protests to the contrary, it really did matter very much to her that he didn't find her attractive, and that maybe it was time to do something about it. Not, she told herself as she switched off the engine and got out of the car, that she actually wanted to attract him. She just wanted to prove to him that he was wrong.

Just a few blocks away was a small shop where she used to buy all her clothes, and she headed in that direction. She hadn't been in there for ages, and for all she knew it might be under entirely different management, but, in the old days when she still cared about her appearance, the woman who owned it always seemed to be able to come up with something just right for her.

Two hours later she emerged from the shop, her arms laden with packages, still a little dazed by what she'd just done, but filled with a delicious sense of satisfaction along with it.

She'd tried on virtually every dress in the store in her size, until she'd finally come up with one that really worked, a cherry-red wool that was perfect, not only for her colouring, but because it moulded her figure like a glove. It was sexy, too, in a dignified way, with long, tight sleeves that buttoned at the wrist, a wide scoop neck that just hinted at the fullness underneath without revealing it, a close-fitting bodice and the skirt a whirl of tiny pleats.

On the premise of 'in for a penny, in for a pound', she'd gone the whole hog, bought everything new, from the skin out. Filmy flesh-coloured silk lingerie, sheer dark stockings, a pair of high-heeled red pumps. Her mother's pearls would set the whole outfit off perfectly.

Then, since she was there anyway, she chose a softly tailored black suit to wear to work, two silk blouses to go with it, another pair of shoes, more lingerie for everyday wear, and ended up by spending more money on clothes in two hours than she had in the past two years.

When she arrived home, Harriet was just hanging up the telephone in the front hall. She gave the packages in Vanessa's arms one sharp glance, but for once made no comment, even though the shop's label was clearly visible on each one.

'That was Robert,' she said.

Vanessa set her parcels down on the hall table and flexed her aching arms. 'Oh? Is he back, then?'

'No. He was calling from Denver. But he will be home on Sunday, just for one day.'

'That's nice.' She picked up the packages again and started towards the staircase. 'I'd better take these things up to my room and get them unpacked.'

There was a short silence, then Harriet spoke again. 'I invited him for dinner Sunday night.'

Vanessa turned around slowly. 'Who?'

'Why, Robert, of course.'

Harriet had that set look to her mouth and chin that meant she was all primed to hold her ground and defend herself against the attack she knew was coming. Vanessa only stood there for a few moments, absorbing this bit of news.

She wasn't thrilled about having Robert and Rees together at the dinner table, especially if she really did go through with her projected image transformation. But, if she made a fuss about it now, Harriet would read more into it than was really there.

'Fine,' she said at last. 'That should be interesting.'

Harriet goggled at her. 'You mean you don't mind?'

'Why should I? Since they're both involved in the business, they're bound to meet sooner or later. It might as well be here.'

When the doorbell rang on Sunday night promptly at seven o'clock, Vanessa was just putting the finishing touches to her face and hair. The dress was so perfect that she'd decided it would be overkill to plaster on a lot of make-up she didn't really need anyway, so she applied just a little powder, a touch of mascara, a pale lip gloss.

She'd snipped at the ragged ends of her dark hair to even it out, then let it hang loose to her shoulders in its natural wave. Rising to her feet, she gazed for a second at her reflection and nodded. It would pass. The dress was alluring, even slightly suggestive, but not in the least cheap or vulgar.

The doorbell chimed again, and from downstairs Harriet's voice floated up to her. 'Would you please get that, Vanessa?' she called. 'I'm up to my ears in clarifying the consommé.'

'All right,' she called back, and started towards the hall.

It had to be Robert, she thought. He had a real fetish for being on time, and somehow she pictured Rees as casually strolling in half an hour or so late, just to prove how cool and superior he was. Maybe he wouldn't come at all. He hadn't really been any more enthusiastic about Harriet's invitation than she was.

As she hurried down the stairs, she wondered how Robert would react to the dramatic change in her. She was rather looking forward to shocking him just a little. He was so used to seeing her in her usual, uninteresting state, casual to the point of dowdiness, that it wouldn't hurt him to see that she actually did have a more feminine side.

But when she opened the door, it wasn't Robert.
Rees Malory stood there under the front porch light,
a long florist's box in his hands. He looked as smooth
and well put together as ever, wearing a dark suit,
crisp white shirt and tie and a tan trench coat with
the collar turned up at the back of his neck.

For a long moment, he simply stared at her. Then
his dark eyes swept swiftly over her from head to toe,
and a slow smile began to form on his lips.

'Well,' he said at last, 'aren't you going to invite
me in?'

'Yes, of course,' she mumbled. 'Sorry. I thought
it was our other guest. Please come in.'

When he was inside, the door shut behind him, he
handed her the florist's box. 'These are for Harriet,'
he said. 'And you, of course.'

'That's very thoughtful of you. She'll be pleased.'
She set the box down on the table and lifted up the
lid. Nestled carefully inside were what looked to be
at least two dozen red roses. 'Thank you, Rees,' she
said with a smile. 'They're beautiful.'

'And so are you, Vanessa,' he said in a low, intimate voice. 'In fact, I can hardly believe you're the
same girl. What have you done to yourself?' He held
up a hand. 'No, don't tell me. I like mystery in a
woman.'

She hadn't a clue how to respond to that, so she
looked away, busying herself replacing the lid on the
box, then held out a hand. 'Here, let me take your
coat.'

As he removed his overcoat, he never once took his
eyes from her, and the suggestive remarks, the close,

steady scrutiny of those penetrating eyes, a sort of steely blue tonight under the glow of the hall light, were making her decidedly uncomfortable. She'd wanted to prove a point to him—that she was capable of attracting him—but by now she was beginning to fear she may have ended up with more than she'd bargained for.

After she'd hung up his coat in the hall cupboard, she picked up the box again, then turned and walked away. 'Let's go into the living-room,' she said over her shoulder. 'There are drinks set out: scotch, vodka, bourbon. Fix yourself whatever you like. I'll just take these into the kitchen and put them in water.'

Just then the doorbell rang again. Robert! She'd forgotten all about him! She stood there for a moment, undecided whether to answer the door or take the roses into the kitchen. She couldn't just leave him standing out there, however, so she set the box back down on the table and went to the door.

When she opened it, he stood there goggling at her for a moment, open-mouthed and wide-eyed. 'Well,' he said at last. 'Hello, Vanessa.'

'Come in, Robert.'

Inside the hall, he gave her another long, appreciative look, then whistled softly through his teeth. 'What in the world have you done to yourself?' he asked in a hushed voice. 'You look——' He broke off, shaking his head. 'I've never seen you looking quite so—so—well, breathtaking is probably the word.'

Then abruptly his gaze shifted past her, and she realised that Rees was probably still standing there. She turned around. He was watching them, his hands hanging loosely by his sides, his mouth crooked in a rather bemused smile.

'Oh, Robert,' she said, turning back to him. 'I'd like to have you meet Rees Malory. You remember, I mentioned that he'd be working with me in the office for a short time.' She darted one swift glance at Rees, then put her arm through Robert's. 'Rees, this is Robert Evans, our company's lawyer—and an old friend of the family.'

Just then Harriet appeared, wiping her hands on her apron, a welcoming smile on her plump face. 'What are you people doing, standing out here in the hall?' She nodded at Robert. 'Hello, Robert. It's nice to see you again.'

'Hello, Harriet,' he said. 'I was just telling Vanessa——'

But Harriet had already gone over to Rees and grasped him by the hand. 'Welcome, Rees. I'm so happy you could make it. Now, let's all go into the living-room and have a drink. Dinner will be ready in half an hour.'

'You go ahead,' Vanessa mumbled. 'I want to get Rees's flowers in water.'

'Flowers?' Harriet cooed, batting her eyes at Rees. 'Oh, Rees, you shouldn't have.' She went over and lifted up the lid of the box. 'Oh, red roses. My favourite. Vanessa, they just match your dress.'

Vanessa snatched up the box from under Harriet's nose, almost knocking her over in the process, and swept out of the room, muttering curses under her breath every step of the way into the kitchen at the way she was falling over Rees! It was sickening! She'd really outdone herself this time. *Two* men!

When she carried the flowers back into the living-room, Rees was making himself right at home at the mahogany sideboard, dispensing drinks, while Robert stood by the fireplace, his elbow on the mantel, looking uncomfortable.

Harriet gave her a bright smile. 'Oh, the roses are lovely, dear. Now, what will you have to drink? I asked Rees to do the honours, since Robert doesn't drink.'

Robert cleared his throat. 'Well, as a matter of fact, I'm allergic to alcohol in any form. It's not a matter of temperance.'

Ordinarily Vanessa didn't drink either when Robert was around. She could take liquor or leave it alone, and it only seemed polite to join him in his absti-nence. But tonight she needed a drink—badly. She wasn't crazy about the idea that Rees was playing host so nonchalantly, but rather than make an issue of it she gave Robert an apologetic smile, and went over to the sideboard.

'What'll it be, Vanessa?' Rees asked cheerfully.

'I'll have a Scotch and soda,' she replied in a loud voice.

Deftly he mixed her a rather stiff drink. When he gave it to her, his fingers just happened to brush against hers. Purposely, she thought, and snatched her hand away so fast that she almost spilled her drink.

'Now,' Harriet was saying, 'let's all sit down and enjoy our drinks.'

They gathered around the fireplace, Harriet in her usual easy-chair, Rees in the chair next to her, while

Vanessa made a beeline for the couch where Robert had settled himself. There was a short silence while they took their first sips, then Harriet turned to Rees.

'I've been wanting to ask you, Rees, what you think of our little business by now.'

Rees darted one brief look at Vanessa, then settled back in his chair and smiled at Harriet. 'Well, I'm only the hired help, you know, just here to learn. But from what I've seen so far, I'd say Vanessa is doing a marvellous job. And she's a fine teacher.'

'Well, isn't that nice?' Harriet cooed. 'Did you hear that, Vanessa?'

'Yes,' Vanessa said curtly, 'I heard.'

'You know,' Harriet went on, ignoring the dark look Vanessa shot her, 'you're something of a mystery man around here. Only the other day my friend Mrs Perkins—back in the hospital again, poor soul—was asking me about you.' She laughed lightly. 'I'm afraid I had to tell her I knew nothing about you.'

Rees stretched his long legs out in front of him, took a long swallow of his drink and set the glass down on the table beside him. 'There really isn't much to tell,' he replied smoothly. 'But I'll be glad to tell you whatever you want to know.'

'Well, for one thing, a fine-looking man like you must be married.'

Vanessa could have sunk through the floor. Leave it to Harriet to get right to the point. She glanced at Rees, whose mouth was twitching with amusement.

'Afraid not,' he said. 'I travel around so much that any kind of home life isn't really in the cards for me.'

'Oh, that's too bad,' Harriet said, lying through her teeth. 'Surely you have a home of your own, though?'

He shook his head. 'Not really. I live pretty much out of suitcases, generally in hotels.'

'Then you don't have any family at all?'

The smile vanished, and his eyes glazed over as his face closed down. 'I have a sister,' he said shortly. He reached for his glass and drained it, then rose to his feet. 'May I pour myself another drink?'

'Of course,' Harriet replied in a subdued voice. She got up from her chair. 'I think I'd better put the finishing touches to the dinner. You have time for just one more.'

To Vanessa's relief, the conversation over dinner was more general. Even Harriet, with her insatiable curiosity, knew when to leave a subject alone, and Rees had made it crystal-clear that any more questions about his personal life were unwelcome. Knowing him, she wouldn't put it past him to flatly refuse to answer, if pressed.

The discussion was mostly on national and international politics, the state of the economy, with a few titbits of local gossip thrown in by Harriet from time to time. Although she made an effort to at least comment now and then, Vanessa didn't have much to say about any of these subjects and remained mostly silent.

As it turned out, she found it comforting to have Robert there, sitting across from her in his usual place, his mild manner and calm, reasonable voice so familiar to her. Rees sat next to him at the foot of the table, and as they talked she would glance covertly from one to the other, watching the two men, who seemed to hit it off right away.

She couldn't help comparing them. They were so different. Robert, with his sandy hair, light blue eyes and drab grey suit seemed so colourless next to the taller, more vibrant Rees. Such thoughts made her feel disloyal. Robert was a wonderful person, an old friend, not some fly-by-night who was here today and would be gone tomorrow. She should be making more of an effort on his behalf.

After the table was cleared and they were drinking coffee, she turned to him. 'How is your case coming on, Robert?'

'Slow,' he replied with a sigh. 'I thought it would be over by now, but the opposing counsel is pulling every delaying tactic in the book.' He glanced at his watch. 'In fact, I really should be going home, much as I hate to. I have a six o'clock flight back to Denver tomorrow morning and still have to repack my bags.'

'Oh, must you leave so soon?' Vanessa asked.

'I'm afraid so.' He pushed back his chair and rose to his feet. 'Thanks very much for the splendid dinner, Harriet,' he said. 'Sorry I have to run off like this.'

Vanessa jumped up from her chair. 'I'll see you to the door.'

They walked together to the entry hall, and after he'd put on his overcoat he turned to her. 'I've been wanting to tell you all evening, Vanessa, how really lovely you look tonight. I can't get over it.' He laughed diffidently. 'I mean, you've always been special to me, you know that, but somehow tonight you've been transformed into a—a—' He shrugged. 'I can't find the right word for it.'

'Well, I gather you like it, anyway,' she said with a smile.

He nodded vigorously. 'Oh, yes,' he said firmly. 'I like it very much.'

His eyes softened then, and he reached out to put his hands on her shoulders, drawing her up against him. 'You know how I've always felt about you, Vanessa,' he said.

'And you've always been special to me, too, Robert.'

Then he bent his head and brushed his lips lightly against hers. It wasn't the first time Robert had kissed her, and although she had no objection neither did any bells ring. She waited, hoping for a more enthusiastic response, but he himself broke it off before it could turn into more than a friendly gesture.

He searched her face for a long moment, as though trying to read what was in her mind, then dropped his hands with a sigh. 'I hate to leave things like this,' he said, moving to the door, 'but now isn't the time or place to do or say what's really on my mind. However, when this case is over and I'm back for good, you and I are going to have to have a serious discussion—about us.'

'Robert——' she began.

'Don't say anything now,' he said, holding up a hand. 'Just think about it while I'm gone. I'll call you from Denver in a few days and let you know how things are going.'

'All right.'

Then he was gone. She stood there for a long moment after closing the door behind him, thinking over the conversation, wondering what she was going to do about it, when all of a sudden she had the eerie feeling she wasn't alone. When she turned around she saw Rees, standing just inside the doorway, not ten feet from her.

He came walking slowly towards her. 'Sorry,' he said. 'I didn't mean to eavesdrop, but it's time I was leaving, too, and since Harriet had something to do in the kitchen she said you'd retrieve my coat for me.'

'Oh, yes,' she stammered, wondering how much of the little farewell scene with Robert he'd witnessed. 'I'll get it for you.'

She got his coat from the cupboard and handed it to him. As he took it from her she felt his hand touching hers, then grasping it and holding it tightly. Startled, she looked up to see him staring down at her, his expression grave, his deep blue-green eyes holding hers in a steady gaze.

'He's a nice guy, your Robert,' he said quietly.

She knew she should remove her hand from his grasp, but somehow she couldn't quite manage it. 'Yes, he is,' she replied in a small voice.

'But he's not for you.'

She frowned up at him. 'What do you mean by that?'

'I mean you wouldn't be happy married to a man like Robert. What's more, you'd end up making him miserable.' He smiled. 'With all that spark and drive in you, you'd eat him alive in time.'

Angrily she tried to tug her hand away, but he held it fast. 'No one said I was going to marry Robert,' she said coldly. 'And, even if I were, I don't see what business it is of yours.'

'Well, let's just say I'm an interested party.'

'And what does that mean?'

'I'll show you.'

The next thing she knew she was in his arms and his warm mouth was pressed very firmly over hers. For a moment she was too shocked to object, and by the time she'd recovered what his hands and lips were doing to her felt so wonderful that her wits seemed dulled to the point of paralysis.

As he tightened his grip on her, holding her closely all up and down the length of his tall, lean body, she sagged against him helplessly. His hands were moving over her back now, lulling her senses, and as his mouth opened slightly over hers she could feel the tip of his tongue against her lips, seeking entrance.

Then, as swiftly as it had begun, it was over. His mouth left hers, his hands slid up her arms to rest on her shoulders, and he stepped back a pace. Her eyes flew open, and she gazed up at him, so stunned by what had just happened to her that she couldn't utter a word. He was gazing down at her, his expression strained, a stray lock of thick dark hair falling over his forehead.

He let her go and ran a hand over his hair, smoothing it back. Then, without touching her, he leaned over and kissed her lightly on the mouth.

'Goodnight, Vanessa,' he said softly.

The next thing she knew he was gone. She stood there, staring at the door he'd just shut, still unable to utter a word, and as she listened to his footsteps echoing down the path she slowly put her fingers on her mouth, which was still tingling from his kiss.

CHAPTER FIVE

THE next morning at breakfast, Vanessa was still trying to erase the memory of Rees's kiss from her mind. He couldn't possibly have meant anything by it. It was merely a display of masculine power, and she certainly was immune to that by now. Harriet and Sandra might consider him the greatest thing to come along since sliced bread, but she was made of sterner stuff. Whatever it was that he'd been trying to prove last night, nothing had really changed between them.

'Well,' Harriet said brightly, breaking into her thoughts, 'I think our dinner went off quite well last night.'

Vanessa gave her a grim look. '*Your* dinner,' she amended. She softened when she saw the hurt look on her aunt's face. 'All right. Yes, Harriet, it went off all right. Actually, it turned out much better than I'd expected. At least they both left early.'

'They're certainly very different men, aren't they?'

'Oh, yes,' Vanessa agreed. 'Same species, but at opposite ends of the spectrum. Something like a tiger and a pussy-cat.'

Harriet choked on her coffee. 'Is that how you see Robert? A pussy-cat?'

'Well, a very nice one.'

'Just don't forget, my dear, that even the tamest tabby has sharp claws.'

86

'What do you mean?'

'Well, I'm not blind. Even Robert must have seen the sparks flying between you and Rees last night. And Robert thinks of you as his property.'

'Well, that's Robert's look-out, isn't it? I've never given him any encouragement or made any promises. And just what do you mean by "sparks" anyway?'

'As I said, Vanessa, I'm not blind. The man is interested in you. Especially,' she added with a sly look, 'with that new dress you had on last night. Very becoming.'

Vanessa felt herself colouring deeply. 'Well, yes, I just thought it was about time I bought some new clothes.'

'And it had nothing to do with the fact that Rees was coming to dinner?'

''Nothing whatsoever.'

'No,' Harriet said mildly, unfolding the morning paper. 'Of course not.'

In spite of herself, Vanessa was oddly pleased that her aunt had noticed Rees's interest in her, as a woman, not an efficient co-worker. Then she suddenly recalled the telephone call from the mysterious Susan. Rees had never mentioned it.

She got up and stretched widely, then stood there for a moment, torn between making what she knew would be a futile attempt to set her aunt straight on the subject of Rees Malory and just letting the whole thing drop in the hope that it would go away.

'Besides, Harriet, even if you're right and he is interested in me, and, God forbid, I entertained

thoughts of getting involved with him, I'm afraid I'd
have to stand at the end of a long line.'

Harriet peered at her from over the newspaper.
'Yes,' she said quietly. 'I'm sure you're right.'
Vanessa's mouth fell open. She'd been expecting a long
rebuttal to her statement. 'But,' her aunt went on,
'I'm sure you could move up fast if——'

'I know,' Vanessa interrupted in a dry tone. 'If I'd
only make an effort. I think I'd better get going to
the office before we get into it over *that*,' she added,
moving towards the door. 'Those tax forms need to
be mailed today.'

'Yes, dear. Have a nice day.'

It was a bright crisp morning, the sun sparkling on
the remains of the snow at the side of the road, the
streets clear. There was even a deceptive hint of spring
in the air, and as Vanessa drove into town she was
still fretting over the conversation with Harriet.

What bothered her was that there was a grain of
truth in what her aunt had been at such pains to imply.
She *had* bought the dress to prove to Rees that she
could be attractive if she tried. And he *had* been
attracted. At breakfast she'd compared him to a tiger.
Now she was beginning to fear that she just might
have that tiger by the tail, without a clue how to
manage it. Certainly taming it was out of the question,
but if she wasn't careful it could devour her.

What did the man want from her? Did he really
have to seduce every woman in sight? 'Well, if so, Mr
Rees Malory,' she muttered under her breath as she

pulled into her parking space, 'you're in for a big disappointment.'

The telephone was ringing in the empty office when she got inside, and she ran to her desk to answer it, shrugging out of her coat as she went.

'Farnham Trucking, Vanessa speaking.'

'Hello, I'd like to speak to Rees Malory, please.'

A woman's voice, a different one this time. Vanessa sank slowly down in her chair.

'I'm sorry, Mr Malory hasn't come in yet. Can I take a message?' She grabbed a pencil.

'No, thank you. I'll try to catch him at his hotel. In case I miss him, would you please ask him to call Janet?'

'Janet,' Vanessa repeated. 'Yes, I'll tell him.'

'Thank you.'

Another one! The man must have a veritable harem! Suddenly she heard a cracking sound. The pencil she'd been holding had snapped in two. Angrily, she threw the pieces in the waste basket. 'This will not do,' she said aloud. Why was she annoyed? What business was it of hers how many women he had on the string?

So he'd kissed her, made her heart flutter just a little. At least she'd had sense enough not to let it progress. He was turning out to be even more like David than she'd imagined at first. Thank goodness she hadn't listened to Harriet. These fascinating men were all alike, so in love with themselves . . .

Fascinating? Was that how she felt about him? She shivered a little at the thought of her narrow escape. She could so easily have fallen into the same old trap if she'd followed her inclinations. Yes, he was fascinating. Good-looking, pleasant, very masculine, with an air of easy assurance. That was part of the trap they set. Well, he could practise his charms elsewhere. It looked as though he had plenty of opportunity.

She left the message from Janet on top of Rees's desk and went out to the garage to check on the day's deliveries.

When she came back to the office, an hour or so later, Rees and Sandra were there, Sandra at her typewriter and Rees sitting on the edge of her desk, leaning towards her with a sheaf of papers in his hands, explaining something to her, while the girl, who was obviously not paying the slightest attention to what he was saying, gazed up adoringly at him.

'Good morning, boss,' he said with a wide grin. He slid off the desk and came walking towards her. 'I've finished the summary of union contracts for the past seven years you asked for. I thought I'd ask Sandra to type it up before I give it to you, if that's all right. Or do you want to look it over now?'

She'd given him the project just last week, asking for a breakdown of drivers' hours and pattern of deliveries, in preparation for the upcoming union negotiations. Somehow she'd had the idea that the job would keep him out of her hair, but she'd never really thought he'd actually do it, much less finish it so quickly.

She always dreaded those union meetings, the lone woman dealing with a group of belligerent men determined to get their own way. She knew they respected her, but it seemed ingrained in them to challenge her authority and it was always a sticky business that left her exhausted. If Rees had done the job right, it would be an enormous help.

'That's great,' she said. 'Sandra can type it as soon as she finishes the tax forms.' She glanced at the girl, whose eyes had never left the tall man. 'Sandra, how are you coming on with them?'

Sandra jumped, then her gaze shifted to Vanessa, as though she'd just now realised she'd come in. 'Oh, hi, Vanessa. What did you say?'

Vanessa sighed. 'The tax forms, Sandra. How are you doing?'

'I'm almost through.'

'Well, when you've finished, Rees has something he needs typed. You can do that next.'

Rees went back to Sandra to continue his instructions, and Vanessa sat down at her own desk, pulling out the list she'd made on Friday of this week's deliveries. As she listened to the patter, watching them out of the corner of her eye, she grew more irritated by the moment at the way the girl looked at him, her eyes devouring him, obviously ecstatic at the close proximity, his smile, his charm.

He was leaning over now, crossing something out on the top page. 'I only hope you can decipher my chicken scratches,' he said with a smile.

'Oh, I think you have lovely handwriting!' the girl cried. 'It's almost like printing and so—so—masculine!'

Rees laughed. 'Well, I don't know about that. But if you have any trouble, just give a yell, and I'll come to the rescue.'

Sandra broke into a fit of the giggles at that, and started making fluttery, embarrassed little gestures with her hands. Determined to ignore them, Vanessa fixed her eyes firmly back on her list. She had barely scanned the first item when suddenly she heard a plopping sound, then a steady 'drip, drip, drip'.

'Oh!' Sandra cried.

Vanessa looked up sharply, filled with a sudden sense of foreboding. All her worst fears were confirmed when she saw that Sandra had indeed knocked over her coffee, which was now spreading in a dark stain across the tax forms she'd just typed.

She leapt to her feet, furious. 'Oh, Sandra! Look what you've done! And they have to be mailed today! How clumsy can you get?'

Rees gave her a sharp look. 'It's my fault,' he said quickly.

By now Sandra had dissolved into a state of blubbering incoherence and, as she watched her, it struck Vanessa that, to be honest, she was far more angry at the easy camaraderie between the two, the affectionate teasing, the girl's obvious worship of the man, the way he managed to charm every female in sight, than she was at the ruined tax forms.

With a valiant effort, she choked back her anger, reminding herself that she was the boss after all. She couldn't afford to let personal feelings interfere with the way she ran the office. Sandra wasn't the world's greatest secretary, but she was willing and did try hard to please.

'I'm sorry, Sandra,' she said at last, forcing out a smile. 'I shouldn't have yelled at you that way. Now, quit crying. It's not the end of the world.'

She went over to assess the damage while Sandra began dabbing ineffectually at the desk top with a tissue, without noticeable success. In the meantime, Rees had gone to the washroom for paper towels and was now down on his haunches, mopping up the mess on the floor.

'There now,' Vanessa said after a cursory examination. 'It's only the last page that's ruined. You can get that done in short order.' She patted the girl's shoulder. 'Come on, Sandra. It's all right. Really.'

When Sandra, subdued and still snuffling, sat back down and started typing, it suddenly dawned on Vanessa that Rees was gone. Just like a man, she thought on her way back to her desk, to disappear at the first sign of trouble. Yet she knew she wasn't being fair. After all, he had cleaned up the floor. What was wrong with her? She was turning into a virago over this man, and she hadn't a clue why.

Half an hour later Sandra heaved a deep sigh, got up from her desk and brought the completed forms over to Vanessa's desk. She stood there silently until Vanessa looked up from her list.

'Everything all right now, Sandra?' she asked, reaching for the forms.

'I think so.' The girl hesitated for a few moments, then blurted out, 'I just wanted to say, well, I'm really sorry about ruining the form, and ever so grateful you weren't mad at me. I think you're a wonderful boss, Vanessa, and I'd like to be just like you some day. You're my role model.'

Vanessa had to smile at the phrase of current jargon. 'Well, I'm not sure that's such an admirable ambition, Sandra, but I appreciate the sentiment. Now you'd better get busy with the typing for Rees. I'd like to see it as soon as possible.'

She didn't get around to reading Rees's report until late that afternoon. The meeting with the union representatives was coming up next week and, now that the tax forms were finally finished, it was time to give those negotiations all her attention.

Sandra had gone home, and Rees was in the garage with the last driver of the day, checking out the cargo. A gentle rain was falling outside, pattering on the roof, but the office was cosy and warm. And very quiet.

As she read, she grew more impressed by the moment. The report was not only concise, informative and covered all the basics, but was so well organised that not a word was wasted. Here was all the data she needed for the meeting—facts, figures, dates—and a great weight was lifted from her mind.

Just as she was finishing up, the door opened and Rees poked his head inside. 'I just sent Jerry off with that last consignment to Salem. If you don't need me for anything else, I might as well be on my way.'

She got up from her chair. 'Just a minute, Rees.' She walked over to him, holding out the report. 'I just wanted to tell you what a great job you did on this. It's going to be an enormous help at the meeting next week.'

He nodded. 'Glad you like it, boss.'

'In fact, I'd like you to attend that meeting with me,' she went on. 'If you're going to learn the trucking business, you might as well be exposed to one of its most difficult aspects.'

'Sure,' he replied, with another nod. 'Be glad to.'

She glanced at her watch. 'Well, I guess it's about that time. Are you ready to leave?'

'Any time.'

She went back to her desk and put the report inside the top drawer, then picked up the jacket from the back of her chair. Rees was still at the door waiting for her, and when she reached him she stopped short.

'Oh, I almost forgot. I have to mail the tax form in.' She laughed. 'After all that fuss this morning, how could I forget?'

'You handled that very well,' he said.

'Oh, not that well,' she said wryly, as she went back to pick up the envelope lying on top of her desk. 'For a minute there I was tempted to throw what was left of the coffee at her.'

'I know. But a lesser boss might have done it. You didn't. You were angry, had every right to be, but you managed to swallow it, soothe poor Sandra, and ended by getting what you wanted out of her with no hurt feelings. That's the way a good manager operates. I'm impressed.'

'Well, thank you very much,' she said, pleased. 'Sandra's a good girl at heart and she tries hard.'

'She worships you, you know,' he said. 'She told me you're her ideal. What did she call it? Ah, yes, her role model. She wants to be just like you.'

'So she said,' she commented lightly as she shrugged into her jacket. 'But as I told her, I'm afraid that's not much of a goal.'

'Why not?'

'Oh, I don't know. It's not important. Shall we go?'

She started towards the door, but he still remained standing there, blocking her way. He was staring down at her, an oddly quizzical expression on his lean face, half-frown, half-smile, as though debating something within himself.

Finally he spoke. 'Have dinner with me tonight, Vanessa.'

She hesitated, tempted, and as she looked up at him she suddenly remembered his kiss, the way his mouth felt on hers, the warmth of his touch. He hadn't mentioned it or referred to it in any way, not even by a look or tone of voice, but she knew with a deep sense of certainty that he was remembering it too.

'Well,' he prompted, 'how about it?'

She shook her head. 'No,' she said. 'I don't think so.'

If he was surprised at her refusal, he gave no indication of it, didn't even bat an eye, except to smile. 'You almost said yes, didn't you?'

'Well . . .'

'Why didn't you? What are you afraid of?'

'Not a thing. I already told you once before. I just don't think it's a good idea to mix business with social life. And, as I recall, you agreed with me at the time.'

'Yes, but I'm flexible. There are exceptions to every rule.' He cocked his head to one side and gave her an

GET 4 BOOKS
A CUDDLY TEDDY
AND A MYSTERY GIFT

Return this card, and we'll send you 4 Mills & Boon Romances, absolutely FREE! We'll even pay the postage and packing for you!

We're making you this offer to introduce you to the benefits of Mills & Boon Reader Service: free home delivery of brand-new Romance novels, at least a month before they're available in the shops, FREE gifts and a monthly Newsletter packed with offers and information.

Accepting these 4 free books places you under no obligation to buy, you may cancel at any time, even just after receiving your free shipment.

Yes, please send me 4 free Mills & Boon Romances, a Cuddly Teddy and a Mystery Gift as explained above. Please also reserve a Reader Service Subscription for me. If I decide to subscribe, I shall receive six superb new titles every month for just £10.20 postage & packing free. If I decide not to subscribe I shall write to you within 10 days. The free books and gifts will be mine to keep in any case. I understand that I am under no obligation whatsoever. I may cancel or suspend my subscription at any time simply by writing to you.

Ms/Mrs/Miss/Mr ⎯⎯⎯⎯⎯⎯⎯⎯⎯⎯ 4A3R

Address ⎯⎯⎯⎯⎯⎯⎯⎯⎯⎯⎯⎯

⎯⎯⎯⎯⎯⎯⎯⎯⎯⎯⎯⎯⎯⎯⎯

⎯⎯⎯⎯⎯⎯⎯⎯ Postcode⎯⎯⎯⎯

Signature⎯⎯⎯⎯⎯⎯⎯⎯⎯⎯⎯
I am over 18 years of age.

Get 4 Books a Cuddly Teddy and Mystery Gift FREE!

SEE BACK OF CARD FOR DETAILS

Mills & Boon Reader Service,

FREEPOST
P.O. Box 236
Croydon
CR9 9EL

No
stamp
needed

enquiring look. 'Tell me, does your rule include your tame lawyer?'

'That's different. I don't work with him every day.'

'Well, after all, I'm only here on temporary assignment. You're such an efficient teacher that I won't be around much longer. Come on, Vanessa. One dinner doesn't mean a lifetime commitment.'

Once again she was tempted, but suddenly something—his tone of voice, his light, bantering approach, just the confident amused look on his face—made her think of David and her old helpless love for him. The similarities between the two men were truly remarkable. And what about Susan? Janet? She had no intention of joining *that* club on the basis of one kiss.

'No,' she repeated, more firmly this time. 'I just don't think it would be a good idea.'

'All right,' he said with a shrug. 'Have it your way.' He pushed open the door. 'Shall we go?'

They walked together out to the car park and got inside their respective vehicles without another word. It rankled that he hadn't pressed the invitation and that, as usual, he'd got in the last word. He was just getting into his car, and on an impulse she rolled down her window and called to him.

'Oh, Rees?'

He turned around. 'Yes?'

She knew she shouldn't do it, but she couldn't help herself. 'I was just wondering,' she said sweetly. 'Did you ask me out to dinner because Susan and Janet are too busy?'

He stared blankly at her for a moment, speechless. Then he shoved his hands in his trouser pockets and came walking slowly over to her. By the time he reached the car, she was already sorry she'd asked such a stupid question. Her heart was quailing within her at what she'd done, but she knew it would be fatal to back down now. She raised her face to his and gave him a defiant look.

He bent over so that his eyes were on a level with hers. 'Why, Vanessa,' he said with mock gravity, 'I had no idea you cared.' She opened her mouth to protest, but he kept on. 'However, since you're so interested, I should tell you that Janet is a woman I worked with in New York, about fifty years old and quite happily married. And Susan is my sister.'

Before she could think up a thing to say, much less splutter it out, he'd straightened up, given her a little salute, and was strolling casually away from her.

She sat there, fuming that he'd won another round, ashamed at herself for forcing the information out of him. But beneath the irritation a glow of pleasure was warming her whole body. Susan was his sister! Janet was middle-aged and married!

Maybe the kiss had meant something to him after all. As she watched the dark Peugeot drive off, she knew one thing for certain. She deeply regretted not accepting that dinner invitation.

Later that evening after dinner, sitting in front of the fire with Harriet, trying to concentrate on her strategy for the upcoming union negotiations while the television blared in the background, Vanessa couldn't keep her mind off Rees.

One minute she was convinced she'd been crazy to turn him down, especially after he'd explained about Janet and Susan. What harm would it have done? It had been a long time since she'd enjoyed an evening out with an attractive man. She'd already made it crystal-clear to him that she wasn't interested in an involvement of any kind. Nor did he seem to want it any more than she did. Was that what rankled?

In the next moment, of course, she was just as convinced she'd done the right thing. He seemed harmless enough on the surface, and perhaps she wasn't involved with other women after all. But there was an air about him, a certain knowing way he had of looking at her, a certain inflexion in his voice that still spelled danger to her.

The shrill ringing of the telephone broke into the stillness just then, and she jumped out of her chair. 'I'll get it,' she called, already on her way, her heart pounding in an eager anticipation she knew was foolish, but couldn't quite repress.

But it was only Robert, calling from Denver as he had said he would, to let her know he'd have to stay at least another two weeks, possibly longer.

'Will you be able to handle the union meeting yourself if I don't get back?' he asked.

'Oh, I think I can manage. Rees prepared a wonderful report for me, a breakdown on past negotiations, and he'll be at the meeting with me for moral support.'

There was a short silence. 'Oh,' Robert said at last. 'I see. Well, that's all right, then. By the way, I'm sorry I haven't had a chance to look into his position with the company yet.'

'Oh, never mind. I think he's just what he says he is, someone sent here to learn about the business for future investment possibilities. If he was a spy or planning to take over Farnham's, I don't think he'd be so helpful or unassuming. I mean, he leaves everything up to me, never interferes, just does whatever I ask him to do—and quite well, I might add.'

'He does seem like a nice enough guy.' There was another, longer, silence. 'Are you interested in him? Personally, I mean.'

'Of course not. Whatever gave you that idea?'

'Oh, I don't know. When I saw him at your place for dinner yesterday——'

'Harriet invited him, not me.'

'Well, whatever. I was just thinking about that red dress you had on, what it did for you—and to me— and wondering if you wore it for his benefit. It was quite a change from your usual style.'

She laughed shortly. 'No, I didn't wear it for his benefit. I just felt like dressing up for a change. Believe me, Robert, I'm immune to men like Rees Malory. Besides, he's not going to be here long enough to make any real impact.'

'He's leaving soon, then?'

'I don't know. He hasn't said for sure, but from the little I know about him he's somewhat of a rolling stone. Anyway, he's not important. Now, tell me, how's the case coming on?'

*   *   *

During the next week, it was business as usual at the office. Rees didn't repeat his dinner invitation, nor did she expect him to. It was just as well, she kept telling herself. As she'd assured Robert, he'd be gone soon anyway.

Finally the day came for the meeting with the union leaders. It was to be held at eight o'clock that evening in the office, and she'd asked Rees to meet her there at seven-thirty to go over their plans.

When the men from the union showed up she introduced Rees simply as a representative from the new parent company, there as an observer. They seemed to be satisfied with that explanation of his presence, and all during the negotiations he sat quietly by her side, without uttering a word.

She'd been a little worried at the beginning when she saw that Victor Channing, a known trouble-maker from way back, was among the union representatives, but everything seemed to be going swimmingly. They were prepared to accept the new increases in hourly wage she had decided on beforehand, and the inclusion of a dental insurance policy along with the medical was met with pleased approval.

Finally, just as they were about to sign the contract, Victor rose slowly to his feet and stood over her. 'I don't know about the others, Vanessa, but there's one thing I'd like to get settled.'

Vanessa steeled herself. 'What's that, Victor?'

'I don't like your using Jim Lake for the odd haul. He's not in the union, you know, and that's bad for morale.'

She knew quite well that morale was the furthest thing from Victor's mind, that he was only interested in asserting his authority, even causing trouble, but she couldn't afford to let him know that.

'Well, Victor,' she said equably, 'as you know, I never do use Jim unless I can't get one of the regular union truckers.'

Victor cocked his head on one side and gave her a knowing look that was not quite a leer. 'So you say. To tell the truth, I'm not so sure. I mean, there couldn't be any *personal* reason you're so set on having him hanging around here, could there? You know he's a married man, don't you?'

As Vanessa stiffened at the totally unfounded accusation, she felt Rees stir beside her, just the merest shuffling of his feet, and she could sense the tension emanating from him. She knew he was preparing to jump into the fray, to leap to her defence, and while this gladdened her heart she knew it wouldn't do.

She flicked a quick sideways glance at him, hoping he would get the message to back off. He met her gaze, raised one dark eyebrow, then set his mouth in a grim line, settled back in his chair and crossed his arms over his chest, glowering darkly.

She turned back to Victor. 'I'm going to forget you said that, Victor,' she said evenly. 'It's not worth discussing, and I think you know that.' Her eyes swept over the other two union men. 'Do either of you have any comment to make?'

They glanced at each other, somewhat red-faced. Then one of them nudged Victor and grinned at Vanessa. 'No. Nothing to say. Don't mind old Vic here. He's got to spout off about something once in a while or he wouldn't feel he'd done his job properly.' They both rose to their feet. 'We're satisfied with the contract as it stands and ready to sign.'

When they'd concluded their business—and they'd parted on excellent terms, including Victor—Vanessa saw them out of the door. She stood there for a moment, watching after them until they were safely inside their car and had driven away. Then she shut the door, slumped back against it with a sigh, and closed her eyes in sheer relief that the whole sticky business was over at last.

When she opened them again, she saw that Rees had risen from his chair and was standing there, gazing at her, a look of concern on his lean face.

'Are you OK?' he asked quietly.

She ran a hand over her hair and pushed herself away from the door. 'I think so,' she said with another long sigh. 'But I could use a drink.'

He grinned. 'I can well imagine. Come on. I'll buy you one. There's a little place just down the street. We can walk.'

She hesitated for the merest fraction of a second, then said, 'That sounds great. Let me just get my coat.'

CHAPTER SIX

THEY locked up the office and walked the few blocks to the nearby cocktail lounge, not speaking along the way. It was a bright, starry, moonlit night, and now that the tense meeting was over Vanessa felt somewhat light-headed, drained of every ounce of energy, but at the same time deeply pleased at how it had turned out.

When they'd been seated at a table and given their order to the waitress, Rees leaned back in his seat and gave her a long, appreciative look.

'Well, I must say, you handled that beautifully, Vanessa. I'm impressed.'

Vanessa laughed. 'Well, thank you. I'm pretty pleased over how it went myself.' She shook her head. 'Although I'll have to admit that for a minute there, when Victor pitched in with his nasty insinuations about Jim Lake, I was afraid I'd lose it and start yelling at him—or worse, burst into tears.'

He nodded. 'I was getting ready to pop him one myself,' he muttered disgustedly. 'What a poor excuse for a man!'

She had to laugh. 'Accusing me of hanky-panky with Jim Lake, of all people! You've met him, Rees. A lovely man, but fat, bald, fifty and happily married.'

He nodded. 'A nice guy, but not exactly every woman's dream, I grant you.'

'Well, I want to thank you for staying out of it, Rees. I mean,' she added hastily, 'I'm glad you were there, in case it got really ugly, but if they once got the idea I needed strong-arm help, I'd never be able to deal effectively with them again, especially after you've gone.'

'I grasped as much when you shot me that "back-off" look.' He laughed. 'I'm afraid I still have trouble stifling my chivalric instincts whenever I see a damsel in distress.' He raised his glass in a toast. 'But I have to hand it to you, Vanessa. You manage very well on your own and obviously don't need a knight in shining armour to come charging to your rescue.'

She wasn't quite sure that was much of a compliment, but decided to take it as one. 'I'm glad you understand. It's the way it has to be if I'm to handle my job properly.'

He took a long swallow of his drink, then gazed at her over the rim of his glass. 'And that's important to you, isn't it?'

'Why, yes, of course it is. I've worked hard to keep the business going after my uncle died. Harriet has no interest in it, never did. In fact, it's still a bone of contention between us that she sold out.'

'It sounds to me as though you view this business of yours as pretty much your whole life.' His tone was casual, but there was a hint of challenge in the deep green eyes. 'Is it really going to be enough for you?'

She stared at him, puzzled. 'I don't know what you mean.'

He shrugged. 'I mean, what about love? Marriage? Children?'

She widened her eyes at him innocently. 'Are you offering yourself as a candidate?'

He gave her an explosive burst of laughter. 'Lord, no!' he exclaimed with real feeling. Then he held up a hand. 'Nothing personal,' he added hastily. 'I just have plans of my own.'

'Plans that don't include love? Marriage? Children?'

He smiled. 'Well, not marriage or children, certainly, not with the way I live. But love is another subject entirely.'

'That's funny,' she said drily. 'Somehow I've always had the impression they all went together.'

He raised a dark eyebrow. 'Not necessarily.'

'Well,' she said with asperity, 'I've gone that route in the past, and ended up with a broken heart and some bitter memories.' She broke off and bit her lip, painfully aware that she'd said much more than she intended. 'But that's ancient history,' she added gruffly with a dismissive wave of her hand.

'Ah,' he said softly. 'I thought there might be something like that lurking in your past.'

'As I said, that's ancient history,' she remarked curtly.

'Well, tell me, then, do your plans include Robert? As a kind of consort?'

She bridled at his tone, which was faintly mocking. 'I doubt it,' she said shortly. She leaned across the table then, and fixed him with a narrow look. 'What about you? You don't mind pumping me dry about my personal life, yet you very skilfully side-step my questions about yours.'

'Do I do that?'

'Yes, you do. Come on, now. Fair is fair.'

'All right, but there really isn't much to tell. I've never been married, and intend to stay that way.' He smiled. 'Like you, my job is pretty much my whole life, and most of the women I've known don't take kindly to playing second fiddle to it.'

She sipped slowly on her drink, waiting for him to go on, but he had fallen silent—clearly he wasn't going to elaborate on his brief reference to his work. If she wanted to know more, she'd have to pry it out of him. Feeling a little giddy from the union meeting and the Scotch she'd consumed rather quickly, she decided to pin him down.

She set her empty glass carefully on the table and gave him a direct look. 'Just what is your job, Rees?'

He shrugged. 'I told you. I work for Global, same as you. They send me out on different assignments, mostly to newly acquired subsidiaries, as a sort of trouble-shooter.' He raised a hand. 'Not that there's any trouble at Farnham's. I just go where I'm sent, to learn, in this case.'

'Sort of a spy,' she remarked coolly.

'No, not really.' He put his elbows on the table and leaned towards her, fixing her gaze on his. 'I'm not your enemy, Vanessa,' he said softly. 'Believe me, I'm on your side.'

He rose to his feet, excusing himself for a moment. As Vanessa's eyes followed him walking away and threading his way around the tables, she was struck by the appearance he made: his fine dark head, his tall, graceful body, his confident walk. A *very* attractive man. Nice, too, she had to admit. He'd said he was on her side. Why not believe him? Just relax and enjoy his company?

Suddenly the little speech he'd made about his chivalric instincts popped into her head. She viewed it with decidedly mixed feelings. She knew she should be glad he saw her as a strong woman, well able to take care of herself, but something still bothered her about that interpretation of her character.

Could it be that deep down she actually wanted to be rescued by that mythical knight in shining armour? And had she been able to handle the situation with Victor tonight so well mainly because Rees was there by her side, ready to jump in if she really needed him?

When he came back, he stood beside the table for a moment, looking down at her. 'Would you like another?' he asked. 'Or are you ready to leave?'

Vanessa debated. She felt unutterably weary by now, and for some reason rather depressed. Reaction, she decided. And she'd already had enough to drink. What she really needed was a good night's sleep.

'I think I'll pass, Rees,' she said, starting to shrug into her coat. 'Right now I just want to get home and crawl into bed.'

He nodded, and called to the waitress for the bill. When Vanessa reached for her handbag, he raised a hand. 'Not this time,' he said. 'This one's on me.'

They walked back to the office in silence, and when they reached her car he waited there while she got inside.

'Well, goodnight, Rees,' she said through the open window. 'And thanks again for everything.'

'My pleasure,' he said.

She turned the key in the ignition and pressed the starter. Nothing happened except for a low whine, emanating from somewhere under the hood. She tried again. This time there was nothing, just a little click, then an ominous silence.

Rees opened the door. 'Move over,' he said. 'I'll give it a try.'

Vanessa hesitated. Then, silently gnashing her teeth, she shifted over to the passenger side, knowing it would be one of those times when all a man had to do was flick his wrist and the machine would obey him.

But it didn't work that way this time. He got the same results that she had. After three abortive tries, he turned to her.

'I'm afraid you've got a dead battery,' he said. 'Do you have jump leads?'

'No,' she said in a small voice. 'But,' she added brightly, 'there must be some in the garage.'

He shook his head. 'For trucks, maybe, but they'd be too powerful for a small car. I'll drive you home, and tomorrow you can have one of the mechanics fix it up for you.'

Although she was slightly put off by his dictatorial tone and bland assumption that she would simply obey his orders, she was too tired to argue with him. Nor did she really feel like going through the trouble and mess of attaching jump leads, even if she could find some that would work.

'All right,' she said, opening her door. 'I can probably borrow Harriet's car to get to work in the morning.'

Inside Rees's car, Vanessa put her head back and closed her eyes. It was only a fifteen-minute drive from the office to her house, but the next thing she knew a hand was on her shoulder, shaking her gently.

'What is it?' she asked groggily. She opened her eyes and looked over to see Rees's face just inches away from hers. 'Where are we?'

'We're at your place.'

She sat up straight and ran a hand over her hair. 'Sorry,' she said. 'I must have fallen asleep. Well, thanks for the lift, Rees. See you tomorrow.' She reached for the door-handle, but before she could open it she heard him speak to her.

'Vanessa.' His voice was low, but with an underlying urgency in it that stilled her hand.

She turned around slowly. 'Yes?'

From the light burning on the porch she could see that although there was a crooked half-smile on his face his eyes were dead serious. They held her so that she couldn't look away from them, and before she could grasp what his intentions were he had reached out a hand and placed it on her face.

'Vanessa,' he said again.

She couldn't move, couldn't think. Her head was in a whirl. All she was aware of was how warm and strong the hand felt on her face, how near he was to her, so near that she could smell his distinctive masculine scent, a clean scent of the outdoors, a lemony soap, a tangy aftershave.

His hand moved slowly from her face to the back of her neck, impelling her gently but inexorably towards him. She couldn't resist, didn't want to resist. With a sigh, she closed her eyes, and the next thing she knew his mouth was on hers, lightly at first, his lips playing with hers, then, slowly, it deepened, became more demanding.

It had been so long since she'd been held this way by a man, his body hard against hers, strong arms around her, large hands stroking gently over her back, and as his mouth opened and his tongue pushed past her lips she met him eagerly, breathlessly, mindlessly, lost in the magic of the moment.

After a long time, he tore his mouth away and pressed his cheek against hers, breathing into her ear. 'Ah, Vanessa,' he whispered. 'I've wanted to do that for a long time.'

He kissed her again, even more hungrily this time, and she gasped inwardly when she felt one hand come around to settle on her breast. As he kneaded the soft fullness gently, teasing, arousing sensations in her which she'd thought were long dead, she knew she was moving dangerously close to the point of no return. If only it didn't feel so wonderful!

He began to fumble at the buttons of her blouse, and when the long fingers slipped inside to touch her bare flesh she stiffened and drew slightly away from him. Immediately the hand at her breast stilled.

'Vanessa?' he said. 'What's wrong?'

She laughed nervously. 'I'm afraid things are moving a little too fast for me, Rees.'

He removed his hand and slowly refastened the buttons. Then he looked away from her, gazing out of the window, sitting quite still, as though struggling for control. She could hear his rasping breath and, as she waited for him to say something, she began to regret what she'd done. What was she so afraid of? She felt bereft at his withdrawal, longed to feel his arms around her again, his mouth on hers, his hands on her body.

But the moment had passed. He slid away from her and reached for the door. 'Come on,' he said. 'I'll walk you to the house.'

The short walk up the path seemed endless. She was in an agony of apprehension, dying to look at him, wishing he would say something, anything. What was he thinking? Had she turned him off for good?

On the porch, she took out her key, unlocked the door, and pushed it open. Then she turned to him. 'Well——' she began.

But he put a finger briefly on her lips, stopping her. 'No,' he said gravely. 'Don't say anything.' He bent down to kiss her lightly on the mouth. 'Goodnight, Vanessa,' he said. 'Sleep well.'

With that, he turned and strode down the path to the car.

Lying in bed that night, she went over and over the scene in her mind. Had she been wrong to let him kiss her, or was her real mistake in stopping him? One thing she knew; she had wanted it to go on and on and on. Nothing she'd ever experienced with David had even come close to the sensations evoked in her by Rees Malory. It was the difference between a callow, selfish boy and a mature man.

Finally, exhausted, she fell into a troubled sleep.

In the morning, the whole thing seemed like a dream. Perhaps it hadn't really happened at all, she thought as she showered and dressed. But she knew it had been real. His kiss still tingled on her mouth, and she could still feel his touch on her breast.

However, in the cold light of day, she was certain she'd been right to stop things before they got out of hand. Whoever this man was, he was light years ahead of her in experience. She hadn't a prayer of coming out of any relationship with him unscathed.

What troubled her now was the fact that she'd have to face him in the office today. She must have been out of her mind last night. She'd managed to break two cardinal rules. Not only had she fallen into the arms of a man who had no intention of making any commitment to her, but it had to be someone she worked with!

She also dreaded having to face her aunt at breakfast. Those gimlet eyes of hers seemed able to probe into the most secret recesses of her heart, and there wasn't a doubt in her mind that Harriet would know the moment she looked at her exactly what had happened.

Steeling herself for the inevitable confrontation, she went downstairs and into the kitchen, where Harriet was sitting at the table, her nose buried in the morning newspaper. After a quick, 'Good morning,' Vanessa sat down across from her to her usual juice, toast and coffee.

They ate in a blessed silence for a while, and Vanessa began to hope she might be able to make a quick getaway after all, when she suddenly remembered the car that wouldn't start.

'Harriet,' she said, 'would it be all right if I used your car today to get to work? Mine conked out on me last night with a dead battery.'

'Yes, of course. I won't be needing it.' She gave her niece a puzzled look. 'But if your car is out of commission, how did you get home?'

'Oh, Rees drove me,' Vanessa replied in an offhand tone.

'I see. Then I take he was at the meeting?'

Vanessa nodded. 'Yes. Since he's here to learn the business, I figured he might as well sit in on it.'

'And how did the meeting go?'

'Quite well. Victor put up his usual fuss, but the others sat on him, and we got the thing signed in short order.'

'Was Rees a help?'

Vanessa laughed. 'Yes, mainly by keeping quiet and letting me handle it myself.'

'I see.' Harriet rattled the paper for a while, then cleared her throat loudly. 'Well, if the meeting went so smoothly, you must have finished early.'

'Oh, yes,' Vanessa replied between bites. 'It was all over by nine o'clock.'

More rattling. 'Hmm, that's funny.' Harriet lowered the paper and gazed at her niece with innocent eyes. 'I could have sworn that it was past eleven when I heard you come home. Did you and Rees go out to celebrate?'

Vanessa gave her a look. 'Harriet, since when have you started checking up on when I get home at night?'

'I wasn't checking up on you!' came the heated protest. 'I woke up and happened to glance at the clock, that's all.' She made a tutting sound. 'My, aren't we touchy this morning!'

Vanessa breathed a deep sigh. 'I'm sorry. I guess I'm still a little jumpy.' She drained the last of her coffee, got up and started towards the door, but halfway there she turned around. 'Do me a favour, will you, Harriet?'

'Of course. Anything.'

'Please back off about Rees Malory.'

Harriet stared at her. 'You're serious, aren't you?' Vanessa nodded. Harriet's round face took on a re-signed, almost sorrowful expression. 'All right, dear,' she said quietly. 'If that's the way you want it.'

'Thanks, Harriet. I really do. Now, I'd better get to work.'

As she drove to the office, still pondering how to handle the meeting with Rees, she tried to picture the various possible scenarios. Would he gloat? Or, worse, come on to her in the office in front of Sandra and the drivers?

Or perhaps his feelings were hurt because in the end she had backed off. Actually, that would be best for her purposes, but a small voice within her told her it was a forlorn hope. Although his self-confidence bordered on arrogance, he didn't seem to suffer from the typical male ego. He wouldn't mind losing a battle or two, so long as he thought he could win the war. It was up to her to make certain that didn't happen.

The best way to handle him, she decided, as she parked Harriet's car next to her own disabled vehicle, was to be brisk and business-like. Pleasant, but cool. Just act as though it had never happened.

Then she noticed that his rented Peugeot was already there in the car park, and her heart turned over. There was no avoiding it. She'd have to face him eventually. She got out of the car, took a deep breath, squared her shoulders, and marched grimly towards the office as though it were the last mile.

If only her heart weren't thudding so hard! It felt as though it would leap out of her chest at any moment. Pleasant, but cool, she reminded herself every step of the way.

But when she reached the door and saw him through the window, her knees went weak and every resolution evaporated. He was alone in the office, leaning forward over his desk, his hands braced on top, studying some papers spread out on it.

That first brief glimpse of him was all it took to remind her that those long arms had held her, the large capable hands had touched her bare skin, the fine mouth had pressed on hers, and he looked so wonderful that it was all she could do to keep from running to him and throwing herself at his feet.

When she finally opened the door and stepped inside, he raised his head, straightened up and looked at her. 'Good morning, boss,' he said. His voice was

pleasant, but cool. 'Have a good rest?' Then he turned
back to his papers.

Her heart sank. He'd stolen her thunder once again!
He was obviously going to ignore *her*! She should have
known. Surely, with his experience, he'd had to deal
with similar situations in the past. Many times, no
doubt. Totally deflated, she stalked over to the clothes
rack and hung up her coat.

'Yes, thank you,' she said. She sat down at her desk
and bent over to open the bottom drawer so he
wouldn't see her face, which she knew must be brick-
red.

Then she heard him walking towards her, and she
raised her head to see him standing there, holding out
the union contract they'd signed last night. 'I've been
going over this,' he said, handing it to her. 'It looks
even better to me this morning than it did last night.
You gave away just enough to keep them happy, but
not so much you won't have anything to negotiate
with next time around.'

She took it from him. 'Yes,' she said stiffly. 'I think
it turned out quite well.'

Their eyes met and, although his manner was still
impersonal, there was a glint in the green depths that
threatened to melt her resolve. But it was too late. His
'pleasant, but cool' manner had taken care of that.

Flushing, she looked away. 'Well, I'd better get
moving if I'm going to get today's shipments out.'

She began shuffling busily through the files she'd
taken out of the drawer, but he kept standing there.
Knowing him, he'd probably stay there all day, waiting
for her to notice him.

She looked up and gave him a bright smile. 'Was there something else, Rees?'

For a second he seemed puzzled. Then his face hardened and his eyes narrowed at her. The seconds ticked by. Gradually the corners of his mouth curled up in a mocking smile. Finally, the smile faded and he nodded briefly.

'No,' he said in a clipped voice. 'Not a thing.'

Watching him as he strode away from her, she felt both relief and regret. Part of her wanted desperately to get up and run to him, to go on from where they'd left off last night. But the sensible part knew she'd done the right thing.

For the rest of the day he seemed as anxious to avoid her as she was him. He spent most of his time out in the garage, talking to the drivers, checking their deliveries, while she busied herself with trivial tasks she'd been avoiding for weeks—straightening files, cleaning out her desk. She even got a start on the January month-end billings.

At five o'clock, Sandra, far prompter at leaving time than she was arriving in the morning, said goodnight and left. Vanessa was alone in the office. As far as she knew, Rees had already gone for the day, too. She hadn't seen him since morning.

She tidied her desk, put on her coat, and locked up the office. It was already dark outside, and as she headed towards her car a light rain began to fall. She sprinted the last few yards, and it wasn't until she had her key out, ready to put it in the door, that she noticed Harriet's car, parked next to hers.

Then it dawned on her. She'd completely forgotten the dead battery! She was supposed to have had one of the mechanics look at it today, and it had slipped her mind completely. Cursing under her breath, she debated what to do, finally deciding that she'd just have to drive Harriet's car home and borrow it again tomorrow while she got her own fixed.

Just then, she heard footsteps coming from the direction of the garage. Her heart leapt. Maybe a mechanic was working late and could fix it after all. But when she looked up she saw Rees just moving into the glare under the lamppost at the edge of the car park. He was walking directly towards her.

When he reached her, she laughed nervously. 'Dumb me, I completely forgot about the car.' She began fumbling frantically in her bag for Harriet's keys. 'Guess I'll have to——'

'I took care of it for you,' he said gruffly.

Her hand stilled. 'Oh,' she murmured weakly. She looked up at him, but in the dim light she could barely make out the expression on his face. From what she could see, it looked pretty grim. 'You mean it's all ready to drive?'

He nodded. 'Give me the keys to Harriet's car,' he said. 'I'll drive it home for you, then you can drop me off back here.'

She wasn't sure she liked that plan, but didn't see that she had much choice. 'All right. Thanks.'

She gave him the keys, and they both set off. As she drove, she tried to think of a way to handle the sticky situation. Here she'd been, avoiding him successfully all day, and now they were thrown together alone in spite of all her careful planning.

At the house he followed her into the driveway, parking behind her. She got out and walked back to Harriet's car, with Rees still at the wheel, the motor idling.

She got inside, and without a word he backed out of the driveway and headed back to town the way they'd come. Although it was only a short drive, the silence began to get on her nerves before they'd gone two blocks. She searched her mind for something to say, but for the life of her couldn't come up with a safe topic.

When they reached the car park, he switched off the engine, then turned to her. 'All right, Vanessa,' he said in a hard voice. 'Let's have it.'

She started to temporise, to play dumb, but it suddenly struck her how childishly she'd been acting all day. Like a giddy schoolgirl, she'd been fluttering around, acting as though nothing had happened last night, avoiding him, yet at the same time annoyed because he'd been cool to her.

She turned to face him. 'All right, Rees. I'm sorry. I've behaved badly. Is that what you wanted to hear?'

'No, it isn't.' His voice was quite calm, but there was an edge to it that told her he was close to anger. 'I want to know why you've been giving me the cold shoulder all day. Were you just playing some kind of game with me last night?'

'Of course not!' she said with feeling. She looked down at her hands, twisting them in her lap. 'I just have had second thoughts, that's all. I mean, it was a mistake, what happened last night. It was my fault,' she added hastily. 'I don't blame you in any way, and——'

'Vanessa!' his voice rang out. Startled, she raised her head. 'Vanessa,' he repeated in a softer tone. 'Look at me.' She did so, and saw him smiling at her. 'Last night was wonderful,' he said earnestly. 'Why do you want to spoil it?'

'Oh, Rees, there are so many reasons I don't even know where to begin. For one thing, we work together, and the two just don't mix. For another—well, you said yourself you'd be gone soon. What's the point of starting something that will be over so quickly?'

He reached out and put a hand on the back of her neck. 'But great while it lasts. Come on, Vanessa.' The pressure on her neck increased, moving her closer to him. 'I want you. I think you want me. We're consenting adults. What would be the harm in enjoying what we can while we can? There's little enough joy to be had in life. Why reject it when it comes along?'

'That sounds pretty cynical.'

'Not at all. Just realistic.'

She raised her eyes to his. The hand kneading the back of her neck was casting its spell over her. Was he right? She did want him. Why should she deny herself what other women took so casually? No one would be hurt. Still, she hesitated.

'I don't know Rees,' she said finally in a troubled voice. 'I just thought...' She waved a hand helplessly. 'I guess it matters to me that people *care* something about each other before...' She broke off again. 'You know.'

'But my darling girl,' he said, pulling her up against him, 'I *do* care.' He tucked her head under his chin and began to stroke her hair. 'Are you trying to tell me you don't care about me?'

She raised her head. 'Oh, no. You know better than that.'

'Well, then?'

She didn't know what to say. What she wanted, of course, was some commitment, even a loose one, some guarantee that she'd even see him again once he did leave. Was that hopelessly old-fashioned? She tried desperately to think it through, but the nearness of him, his familiar scent, his hard body next to hers confused her. She couldn't think. All she knew was that she wanted him.

Then suddenly, out of the blue, an image of David rose up in her mind. This was exactly the way she'd felt with him. The only difference was that he'd made promises, while Rees wasn't committing himself to anything. He might not be willing to offer her what she wanted, but at least he wouldn't deceive her.

Still, that reminder of her old heartache sobered her. She pulled out of his arms, and slid away across the seat. He made no effort to hold her, but she knew he was waiting for an answer.

'I've got to think about it, Rees,' she said at last. 'I need some time.'

He didn't say anything for a moment. Then, 'Sure,' he said. 'I understand. Believe me, I'm not trying to talk you into anything you don't want. And I'm damned if I'll beg.'

He opened the door then, and the minute he was outside she started up the engine again and drove off quickly, before she could change her mind.

The ball was now firmly in her court. He was leaving the decision entirely up to her. Although nothing had actually been resolved, at least she felt more in control, and that night she slept like a log—so well, in fact, that she didn't wake up until eight o'clock.

It was past nine when she got to the office. Rees and Sandra had already arrived and were just taking off their coats, laughing and joking as usual, when Vanessa walked in the door. They said good morning and, while Sandra went out to put on the coffee, Rees came over to her desk and smiled down at her.

'How are you this morning, Vanessa?' he asked softly.

She returned his smile. 'Just fine. And you?'

'Couldn't be better. Except that I'd like to kiss you.'

She flushed, pleased, and laughed lightly. 'Not right here in the office, I hope.'

He waggled his eyebrows. 'OK, boss. Later, then?'

She laughed again. 'Maybe.'

'Come on, don't keep me in suspense.'

Just then Sandra came back with the coffee, and the three of them settled at their desks. The little by-play with Rees had unsettled her again. His presence was too overpowering for her. She couldn't think while he was around.

With an effort, she turned to the mail on her desk, which Sandra had picked up on her way to work. At the bottom of the pile was a creamy envelope with the familiar Global Enterprises logo on it, addressed to her personally. She slit it open and began to read:

> Dear Ms Farnham, It has come to our attention that a convention of trucking companies will be held in Santa Barbara, California on the fifteenth and sixteenth of February. We here at Global are pleased with the performance of your company, but in the interests of good relations within the industry would like very much for you to attend.
>
> In anticipation that you will agree, we have made a reservation for you in advance at the Mirador Hotel in Santa Barbara for those dates.

It was signed by one of the vice-presidents of the company.

Her first reaction was that she couldn't possibly go. She couldn't spare the time away, she hated conventions, had always avoided them in the past. On the other hand, the dates mentioned were on a weekend— next weekend, in fact—and it might be a good idea to get away from everything, Rees included, give her a chance to sort out her feelings about him.

Before she could change her mind, she got up from her chair and cleared her throat loudly. Rees and Sandra looked at her. She held up the letter.

'Looks as though I've been summoned from on high to attend a convention in Santa Barbara next weekend,' she announced.

'Ooh,' Sandra squealed. 'Lucky you. California in February. Sounds heavenly. Are you going?'

'Yes. I don't think I have much choice.'

Rees rose slowly to his feet. 'That's interesting,' he said, holding up an identical sheet of paper. 'I received the same summons. Looks as if we'll be going together.'

CHAPTER SEVEN

VANESSA stared at him, speechless. Before she could even gauge her reaction to this startling bit of news, Sandra had broken in excitedly.

'Oh, isn't that wonderful!' she gushed. 'Now you can go together.' She wrinkled her nose in disgust. 'Heck, you guys have all the luck. Wish I could go to California in February. I've never even been out of Oregon.'

By the time she'd wound down, Vanessa had collected herself enough to speak. 'Well,' she said briskly, 'we'll see about that. I don't know if it's such a good idea for both of us to be gone at the same time.' Since she'd got along quite well before Rees came, she knew this was a feeble excuse, but she felt she had to say something, just to temporise while she digested the news.

'But it's a weekend!' Sandra protested.

'Yes. So it is.'

Throughout this exchange, Rees hadn't said a word. Vanessa looked at him now. He was leaning back against his desk, hips braced on the edge, the fateful letter still dangling in his hand. There was a bemused expression on his face, as though he was waiting for her to come to a decision.

'Rees,' Sandra chimed in, turning to him. 'Tell her she has to go.'

He shrugged. 'She's the boss. It's up to her.'

They both looked at her. 'Well,' she said at last, tossing the letter on top of the desk, 'we don't need to decide this minute.' She turned to Rees. 'You at least should probably go, Rees. Since you're here to learn the business,' she added drily.

His eyes widened at her, and the moment the sarcastic words were out she regretted them. It wasn't his fault that the company had done this. He had no more control over their decisions than she did. It was only her suspicious nature coming to the fore again.

She smiled. 'We can decide later.' She sat back down at her desk. 'Right now we'd better get to work.'

Sandra had a dental appointment that afternoon, and the moment she left Rees came over to Vanessa's desk and stood there, staring down at her.

'Well,' he said. 'What do you think by now?'

She looked up at him. 'About the trip?' she said. He nodded. With a sigh, she leaned back in her chair. 'I don't know. Since our masters have requested it, I probably should do it.' She frowned. 'But——'

'But you're not so hot on the idea of my going along with you,' he supplied.

She shrugged. 'I guess so.'

He braced his hands on top of her desk and leaned towards her. 'We could have a good time,' he said softly.

As she met his gaze, her bones seemed to be turning into jelly. His face was so close that she could see the day's stubble on his cheeks and chin, the way the little lines around his eyes crinkled when he smiled. She remembered how that fine mouth had felt on hers. This supremely attractive man wanted her. She wanted him.

'I guess it depends,' she finally said in a low voice.

He quirked an eyebrow. 'On what?'

'On what it would mean. Your expectations.'

He straightened up and smiled down at her, an amused glint in his eyes. 'My hopes are not the same thing as my expectations. You know what I want. But it's entirely up to you. In any case, I see no reason why we shouldn't take advantage of a weekend in Southern California, even if we end up not even speaking to each other.'

Still she demurred. 'I don't know, Rees.'

'What are you afraid of, Vanessa? You should know by now I'm not going to force myself on you. If you have doubts about that, let me assure you——'

'No,' she said, waving a dismissive hand in the air. 'It's not that.'

'Well, then?'

She gave him a long, careful look. 'I'll think about it.'

On the following Friday evening, Vanessa found herself on a plane winging its way south to California.

It had to be fate, she thought as she glanced over at Rees out of the corner of her eye. He was sitting beside her quite calmly, taking it all in his stride, his nose buried in the prospectus for the convention. But then he had been calm about it right from the beginning.

Now the problem of what to do about him had simply been taken out of her hands, and here they were, the two of them, off on a weekend together. Part of her was thrilled to the core, filled with a wild kind of anticipation, but at the same time she was apprehensive. Was she really ready for this? And was he simply taking it for granted that they'd end up in bed together? Perhaps even share a room?

After she'd made up her mind to go, she'd been so flustered, buying new clothes—summery outfits for a warmer climate—that she hadn't even bothered to investigate the details. Now she wished she had. The closer they got to Santa Barbara—just a short trip from Oregon, under an hour—the more nervous she became about what might lie ahead.

Harriet, of course, had been delighted but, true to her word, hadn't made the slightest suggestion that there could possibly be a personal element in the trip, just said she was glad Vanessa was finally going to take a short holiday from work.

Just then Rees reached over and took her hand. 'How're you doing?' he asked.

She looked at him. 'Great. I've never been to Santa Barbara before.' She laughed. 'In fact, I've never even been to California. I suppose you have.'

He nodded. 'Many times. In fact, I was born there. The climate is great, but the hordes of people who swarm there every year have just about ruined it.'

'Did you grow up there, too?'

He nodded. 'In a little town called San Luis Obispo, just up the coast from Santa Barbara. You've probably never heard of it.'

'But you don't live there any more?'

'No. Not for many years.'

'I know you travel a lot in your work, but you must have *some* kind of home base.'

'You know, I really don't. As I mentioned before, I have no family to speak of, just a sister, Susan. In fact, she still lives in Lompoc, not far from Santa Barbara. I plan to visit her this weekend.' His hand tightened on hers. 'I hope you'll go with me.'

She grinned. 'What about the convention?'

He waved his other hand in the air. 'Oh, we'll show up and sign in, to keep Global happy, but I see no reason to attend all those dreary functions. Do you?'

She shook her head. 'Can't think of one.'

When they checked into the hotel, she was relieved to discover that they had separate rooms. Although she'd pretty well made up her mind what was going to happen between them this weekend, she wanted it to be natural, to just happen. It would have been just a little too crass for her taste to share a room.

When the bellboy conducted them up to the third floor, however, and she realised that their rooms were connecting, with a large bathroom between them, she froze. But Rees hadn't made the reservations, after all. It couldn't possibly have been his doing.

Alone in her room, she went to the window and gazed out at the wide, sandy beach, the enormous stretch of the Pacific Ocean beyond it. The sun had set, and it was growing dark, but there was a bright moon, and the air was balmy compared to the frigid temperature she'd left behind in Oregon.

Just then there came a knock on the connecting door. She went over to open it, and Rees stepped inside. He'd taken off his jacket and tie and rolled his white shirt-sleeves up to his elbows. They stood there for a moment, facing each other, their eyes locked together, and when he reached out for her she moved into his arms.

'Mmm,' he said, nuzzling her neck. 'You smell wonderful.'

She raised her arms up around his neck and smiled up at him. 'Mmm,' she mimicked. 'So do you.'

He gazed down at her for a long moment, then his arms tightened around her as he pulled her closer up against his long, lean body. His head bent towards her, and she closed her eyes, filled with a delicious sense of anticipation.

His mouth came down hard on hers, and before long she could feel his warm breath on her cheeks. His hands moved up and down her back, sliding on the thin material of her silk blouse. She opened her mouth to his probing tongue and pressed closer to him, intensely aware of his hard arousal against her thigh.

His hand was on her breast now, moving back and forth across the fullness, his fingers lingering over each aroused peak. In a moment he began to move forward, his long legs pressing against hers, propelling her backwards towards the bed in the centre of the room, until the edge of it buckled the back of her knees.

But when he bent over her, easing her down on the bed, she began to panic. She wasn't ready for this. It was too soon. They'd just arrived. She needed time to get her bearings. She put her hands on his chest and pushed him away, then slid her body out from under his and jumped off the bed.

'Vanessa?' he called to her. 'What's wrong?'

She was at the window, staring out blindly at the blinking lights along the beach, her hands clenched at her sides, shaking from head to toe. It had been a mistake to come. He was pushing her into something she wasn't prepared to go through with. Not just yet.

He came up behind her and stood there, not touching her. 'What's wrong?' he asked at last in a low voice.

'I'd like to be alone now, if you don't mind,' she finally managed to croak out in a shaky voice.

'Vanessa!' he said sharply. 'Turn around and look at me.'

When she didn't move, he put his hands on her shoulders and forced her around so that she had to look at him. In the dim lamplight, his face was livid, the lines deeply etched, his mouth set in a harsh line, his eyes blazing emerald fire.

'Just what kind of game do you think you're playing here?' he demanded. 'You turn hot and cold on me like some damned chameleon. I'm not made of stone, you know.'

By now she was growing angry herself. 'You may recall,' she said heatedly, 'that at one time you made me a solemn promise you wouldn't push me into anything I wasn't ready for. Somehow I got talked into this trip, and then when I get here find we have conveniently connecting rooms.'

He crossed his arms in front of him and glared at her. 'I see,' he snarled. 'And that's my fault, I suppose. What do you want me to do? Change my room?'

'And then,' she went on, ignoring him, 'before I have a chance to absorb that bit of news, you come charging in here like—like——' she sputtered, unable to go on.

'Like what?' he demanded. 'It didn't seem to me you were putting up much resistance a few minutes ago. Not until it was time to follow through, that is.' He shook his head in disgust. 'I've had more than enough experience with teases to last a lifetime, and, if that's what you're trying to do, let me tell you it won't work.'

'I am *not* a tease!' she cried. 'You have no right to say that. I never made you any promises. You're just so used to getting your own way with women that your ego can't take a refusal.'

She stamped her foot and whirled around to face the window again, rigid with fury. Behind her, she could hear his laboured breathing, and knew he was having trouble holding his own temper in check.

After a moment she heard his footsteps moving away from her, the connecting door opening, then slamming shut.

She threw herself down on the bed and burst into tears.

Her first impulse was to turn right around and catch the next flight back to Oregon, but when she realised that meant she'd have to face Harriet's grilling, she decided to stick it out. With luck, she'd be able to avoid him. Since he'd said he planned to visit his sister, he obviously had no intention of attending any of the convention functions, so she'd be safe enough there.

The next morning, then, she repaired the ravages of the previous night as best as she could and went down to the dining-room for breakfast. There hadn't been a sound from Rees's room either last night or this morning. Perhaps he'd changed his room.

The thought that had kept her tossing and turning all night was still there in the morning. *Was* she a tease? Surely not. There had been nothing calculated in her behaviour. She'd only reacted instinctively, in a blind panic.

It didn't really matter. She'd lost him now for good, anyway. And even if she could honestly convince herself that she hadn't been playing with him, she knew she'd handled it all wrong. In fact, she probably owed him an apology. But it was too late for that, too.

She was just getting up from the table when she saw him come in. She looked around for a place to hide, but he was coming straight towards her in his typical long stride, his face set and grim. All she could do was stand there and wait for him.

'Sit down,' he said when he reached the table. 'I want to talk to you.'

She sat, and as he took the seat across from her she glanced at him warily, wondering what was coming. Last evening's battle seemed to have left its ravages on him too, and he looked as though he hadn't slept any better than she had. His face was drawn, his eyes glazed over, and the lines around his eyes and mouth deeper.

'First,' he said, 'I want to apologise for the things I said to you last night. I was angry—hurt and disappointed, too, I guess—and frustrated out of my mind.' He made a stab at a smile. 'You can be very maddening, you know, when you set your mind to it.'

'Well, I'm sorry, too,' she said. 'I don't know what got into me. It just suddenly seemed more than I could handle. But Rees,' she reached out a hand that didn't quite touch him and peered earnestly into his face, 'I'm not a tease. You've got to believe that.'

He nodded glumly. 'I know that. It just seemed like it in the heat of the moment.' He smiled at her again, this time more warmly. 'Anyway, can we forget last night and just concentrate on enjoying ourselves for these few days? Just as friends,' he added hastily. 'I mean, I like you, Vanessa. I enjoy your company. And if you'd like, I'll get my room changed.'

She laughed. 'Oh, don't bother.' She gave him a sly look. 'I'll just keep my door locked.'

'I'm sure you will,' he commented in a dry tone. 'Now. After breakfast, will you come with me to visit my sister? I've arranged to rent a car, and it's only a short drive.' His eyes took on an amused glint. 'Or do you want to attend the seminar?'

'No,' she replied happily. 'I think I'll pass.'

He had rented a convertible—almost mandatory in California—for the drive, and as they drove along the coast through the small towns on the way north, the warm breeze blowing, the sun beating down on them, Vanessa felt happier, more light-hearted, than she had in years.

In fact, terrible as it was at the time, last night's battle seemed to have acted as a sort of catharsis. In some way she didn't quite understand, a lot of old ghosts had been laid to rest, simply by her shouting at him. And the fact that *he* had come to her to apologise made the whole episode worthwhile.

'Tell me about your sister,' she said. 'Is she like you?'

He laughed explosively. 'I hope not! No, she's a much nicer person.'

'Younger?'

He nodded. 'Five years.'

'Let's see,' she teased. 'That would make her about forty.'

'Hey!' he protested. 'Take it easy. I'm not even there yet myself.'

'Oh, sorry.' She examined his profile carefully, strong and clean against the blue of the sea and sky. 'I thought I noticed a few grey hairs. There,' she said, pointing to a spot just above his ear where there were indeed a few silver strands sprinkled among the dark hair.

He raised a hand off the wheel to rub the spot, and gave her a quick, rueful smile. 'Ah, well. It comes to all of us in time.'

'About your sister,' she continued. 'Is she married? A career woman?'

'Neither,' he said in a clipped voice.

They had reached the outskirts of Lompoc now, and he slowed the car to a crawl. At the stop light on the main street, he turned to her, his eyes troubled, his forehead creased in a frown.

'I guess I should tell you about Susan before we get there.' The light changed, and the car moved forward. 'She's not well. The place we're going to is a nursing home.' His eyes flicked back at her briefly. 'She has a form of multiple sclerosis.'

Vanessa was struck dumb. She couldn't think what to say to him. The pain in his voice tore at her heart, and for a moment all she could do was stare wordlessly at him. His eyes were fixed firmly on the road ahead, his mouth set in a grim line.

'Oh, Rees, I'm so sorry,' she faltered at last.

'She's in remission now,' he said in a more cheerful tone. 'And she's very brave about the whole thing. But she's at the point where she does need looking after. It's a strange disease, very unpredictable, and affects different people in different ways.'

'How bad is she?' she asked quietly. 'I mean, you said she was in remission.'

'You may know that MS is basically caused by lesions in the spinal cord that flare up, then heal, but she does have some permanent damage. By remission I mean that it hasn't progressed for a long time. She's confined to a wheelchair and her speech is somewhat slurred, but as I say it's an unpredictable disease. The doctors say she could get up and walk tomorrow. In the meantime, she needs care.'

'How long has it been since you've seen her?'

'Oh, I try to get down just about every weekend.'

She stared at him. So that was where he went every Saturday! Here she'd had visions of romantic interludes, flaming love affairs with glamorous women, and all along he'd been visiting his sister!

They were on a winding road now that led up into the low foothills, which were heavily forested and bright with a few early wild flowers, purple and pink. After a while they came to an open iron gate and drove through on to a paved road. On either side stretched well-tended green lawns and flower beds in full bloom.

He parked in front of a low pink stucco building with a red tile roof that looked more like a Spanish hacienda than a nursing home, and they went inside to a wide, spotless lobby where a few people milled around, some in wheelchairs, some on crutches.

Just then a lovely girl with long blonde hair wheeled towards them. 'Rees!' she cried. 'You did come.'

He bent down to kiss her lightly on the cheek and left his hand on her shoulder while he turned to Vanessa. 'Susan, I'd like you to meet a friend of mine, Vanessa Farnham. She also happens to be my boss, so be nice to her. Vanessa, this is my sister, Susan.'

'I'm so happy to meet you, Vanessa,' the girl said. 'Rees never brings any of his friends to see me.' She started to wheel off. 'Come on, I'll give you a quick tour.'

The whole place—grounds, building, interior—reeked of money, and as they wandered around Vanessa wondered how Rees could afford to keep his sister here on his salary. Perhaps there was a rich relative in the background somewhere, or maybe they had inherited money from their parents.

*   *   *

Afterwards, they decided to drive into town for a late lunch at a small restaurant on the beach. Vanessa watched as Rees lifted Susan up to set her in the car, then collapsed the wheelchair and put it in the back seat, all his movements deft and practised, as though he'd performed them many times in the past. Vanessa got in beside Susan, and they drove off.

Vanessa didn't have much to say during lunch, but was content to let the brother and sister chatter, mainly about Susan's progress and the things she was able to do. The outing was obviously a real treat for the girl, and there wasn't a hint of self-pity in her tone, nor pity for her in Rees's.

At one point she turned to Vanessa. 'I'm sure all this must be terribly boring for you, Vanessa. I'm always so glad to see Rees that I'm afraid I get carried away.'

'Not at all,' Vanessa reassured her. 'I'm enjoying myself immensely. Especially the scenery. I love the ocean, and I still can't quite get used to seeing flowers blooming in February.'

'I've never been to Oregon,' Susan said. 'What's it like?'

Vanessa laughed. 'This time of year, not much. But it is lovely in the summer, and I rather like the change of seasons.'

'Yes, California sunshine can get boring.'

Back at the nursing home, Rees excused himself and left the two women alone for a while.

'He's going to check with my doctor,' Susan said, rolling her eyes. 'He's such a worry-wart about me. He knows they won't have anything new to report.'

'He obviously loves you very much,' Vanessa said softly.

Susan gave her a brilliant smile. 'Yes, I think he does. I mean, he's so faithful about coming to visit me whenever he can, and never makes me feel he's doing it out of a sense of duty.'

'I'm sure he isn't.'

They were in Susan's large room, which looked more like a sitting-room or studio than a hospital bedroom. There was a low bed covered in batik in a small alcove, but most of the space was filled with artefacts of Susan's many interests. A drawing-board by the window, a typewriter on a desk, a lovely flower arrangement on one table, books piled on another.

There was a short silence as Vanessa examined the water-colour on the drawing-board, and when she came back to sit next to Susan on the low couch the girl gave her a hesitant look.

'I hope you won't think I'm getting too personal, Vanessa,' she said at last, 'but I've been wondering ever since you came just how serious your relationship is with Rees. I mean,' she added hastily, 'since you're the first friend he's ever brought here, I kind of assumed that you were something special to him.'

Vanessa flushed. 'Oh, I'm not so sure about that. We work together, and enjoy each other's company, but,' she smiled, 'I don't think your brother is in the market for a permanent companion.'

Susan sighed. 'Oh, drat him and his mania for independence anyway!' she exclaimed. 'I've been telling him for years that he should settle down, but he only passes it off. I think he'd make a wonderful father.' She laughed. 'Oh, I know he has his faults, but he's my brother and I love him. And underneath that rather arrogant exterior, he's really a very caring man who feels things deeply.'

'Yes,' Vanessa said slowly. 'I can see that. But I guess it's really up to Rees what he wants to do with his life.'

'But I think you do care about him,' Susan went on eagerly. 'And I can tell he cares about you. He wouldn't have brought you here otherwise. He's such a private person, even with me.'

Rees himself appeared in the doorway just then. He stood there for a moment, looking from one woman to the other, then smiled and stepped inside.

'Been gossiping about me?' he asked lightly.

'Oh, the vanity of the man!' Susan cried. 'What makes you think you're so interesting?'

He came to stand beside her and put a hand on her smooth golden hair, ruffling it playfully. 'You always did know how to put me in my place, little sister,' he said fondly. He looked at Vanessa. 'If you're ready, I think we'd better hit the road. Don't want to tire Susan out.'

'Oh, I'm not tired,' the girl said.

But, looking at her, Vanessa could see that there were circles under her eyes that hadn't been there when they'd arrived, and her thin shoulders sagged forward.

She'd also been having more and more trouble with her speech as the afternoon wore on.

'Yes,' she said, rising to her feet. 'I'm ready.'

They hardly spoke at all on the way back. Vanessa knew somehow that Rees wanted to be alone with his thoughts. He'd been the soul of light-hearted joking and teasing all day, but underneath she could sense a sadness over his sister's condition that he couldn't quite hide. At least, not from her.

It was growing dark by the time they arrived back in Santa Barbara, and Rees had put the top down against the chill of the early evening. A light fog was rolling in off the ocean, and he focused all his attention on his driving.

She was just as content with the silence. What she'd seen today had altered her view of Rees Malory dramatically, revealed depths to his character that she hadn't dreamed existed. He certainly no longer seemed like the shallow womaniser she'd been so afraid to trust. His concern for his sister had been genuine, and it must cost him a great deal to hide that concern from Susan so well.

She thought, too, about their brief conversation while Rees had been speaking to the doctor. Was she special to Rees? His sister seemed to know him quite well, probably better than anyone else on earth, and she thought so. But what that meant with regard to their relationship she hadn't a clue. Her own feelings were so confused by now that she didn't really know how she felt about him, except that she respected and admired him a lot more now than when they'd set out that morning.

'What do you think?' he said as he parked the car. 'Should we break down and attend the banquet tonight?'

'I suppose it's the least we could do,' she replied with a smile. 'We should have something tangible to report to Global, since they paid our way down here.'

He glanced at his watch. 'Well, it's only a little past five, and the dinner is scheduled for eight o'clock. Is there anything you'd like to do in the meantime?'

'No, I don't think so. Actually, what I'd really like is a short nap. I didn't sleep too well last night.'

He gave her a long look. 'No,' he said at last. 'Neither did I.' She was certain then that he was going to reach out for her, and she wondered what she would do about it. But all he did was put a hand lightly on her cheek, then withdraw it quickly. 'Thanks for coming with me today, Vanessa. It's always hard for me to see her like that, and it helped to have you along.' He reached for the door handle. 'Now, shall we go?'

In her room, Vanessa removed the cotton blouse and skirt she'd worn that day, and lay down on top of the bed. Her feelings were so stirred up that she was certain she'd lie there wakeful until it was time to get dressed for dinner, but the moment her eyes closed she began to drift off.

Some time later she was awakened by a loud commotion down in the driveway in front of the hotel: car doors slamming, a horn tooting, loud laughter.

She jumped up with a start and turned on the bedside lamp. Blinking in the sudden glare, she glanced at her watch. It was past seven! She'd slept for two hours, and she just had time to get ready for the banquet.

After a quick shower, she put on her short silk robe and went to the cupboard where she'd hung the few clothes she'd brought along. She'd bought a new dress for the trip: a pale blue summery dress for a warmer climate, of the thinnest silk, with tiny straps over a straight, low-cut bodice.

Now, gazing at it, she wasn't so sure it was such a good idea. How could she justify fending off Rees's lovemaking, then appear in such a seductive outfit? That *would* be teasing. She'd wear the black crêpe. With a little jewellery, it could go anywhere.

Just then there was a discreet tapping on the connecting door. Without thinking, she called, 'Come in.'

She heard the door open, and looked up to see Rees standing in the doorway. All he had on was a pair of dark trousers and a white shirt, unbuttoned, to reveal a broad expanse of smooth, bare, well-muscled chest. He was fiddling with the cuff of one sleeve, frowning down at it.

'Vanessa,' he said, walking towards her. 'Do you suppose you could help me with this cuff-link? I never could fasten the damn things and——'

He broke off just as he raised his eyes. He stood there as though rooted to the spot, staring, and it wasn't until then that she suddenly realised all she had on was the thin silky robe. They were only a few feet apart now, close enough so that she could see the drops of water glistening on his dark hair, the tiny nick on his chin where he'd shaved, and smell the lemony scent of his aftershave.

Instinctively she raised a hand to clutch the openings of the robe together, but something told her it was far too late for that. He looked so wonderful, so appealing, standing there with his hair still tousled from his shower, that all she knew was that she wanted this man, especially after seeing him today with his sister. In a flash she realised that the worst had already happened. She was in love with him.

The next thing she knew she was in his arms. Whether she'd taken the steps or he had it didn't matter. She clung to him mindlessly, wordlessly, ready to give him anything he wanted from her, knowing she wanted it, too. The future no longer mattered.

Suddenly his body tautened against hers, and he put a hand under her chin, tilting her head back so that she had to look up into his eyes.

'Are you sure?' he asked in a low voice.

She didn't trust herself to speak. All she could do was nod. His hold on her tightened then, and his mouth came down on hers.

CHAPTER EIGHT

AT FIRST Rees's lips brushed only lightly, tentatively over hers, as though testing her response, but when she sighed deeply and melted against him she heard him draw in his breath sharply, and the kiss deepened. His arms tightened around her, drawing her closely to his long, hard body.

After a moment he tore his mouth away and, placing light, lingering kisses on her face, her eyes, her chin, pressed his lips at her ear, his smooth, freshly shaven cheek on hers.

'I want you, Vanessa,' he groaned. 'Put your arms around me. Touch me.'

She slid her arms eagerly up around his neck. Then his mouth was on hers again, more insistent this time. She felt his tongue against her lips, seeking entry. Her lips parted, and she gasped as it invaded her mouth. He tasted of toothpaste, a clean, heady taste that filled her with desire.

His hands were moving over her back, the thin silky material of her robe sliding sensuously on her bare skin. His touch was firm and sure and, as his warm hands travelled over her rib-cage, brushing against the sides of her breasts, all thinking ceased.

He pulled at the ties of her robe and slipped it off her shoulders. One hand came back to settle at the base of her neck, warm and soft on her bare skin.

She gasped as she felt it drop lower, moving now over one aroused breast to the other, his fingers playing lightly, teasingly.

Then his lips left hers and he pressed them against her neck, her collarbone, her breast, leaving a trail of fire until they closed moistly over one taut, thrusting peak. She raked her fingers through his crisp dark hair and threw her head back, lost in a mindless state of sheer ecstasy.

She'd never known lovemaking could be like this. Her whole body seemed to be a quivering mass of pure sensation. All she was aware of was Rees's hands and mouth on her body, his ragged breathing. The frantic potency of his unleashed passion overwhelmed her. Gone was the controlled, confident façade, to reveal a man transported, burning with desire, worshipping her flesh.

When he released her momentarily to shrug his shirt off, she clutched blindly at him, her hands roaming over the smooth, bare chest, the hard muscles of his arms and shoulders, and, when he came back to her, crushing her to him, she moaned deep in her throat and moulded her body to his with a wild longing.

His hands slid down to her hips, pulling her lower body against his, his need for her unmistakable, sure proof of her power over him. She looked up into his eyes. In the dim light of the lamp burning by the side of the bed, she could see the fire in the deep green eyes, the broad chest heaving as he struggled for control.

'Now, darling,' he rasped. 'Now.'

'Oh, yes, Rees,' she said. 'Now.'

Slowly, his arms still tight around her, he began to move towards the bed, his strong thighs guiding her steps as if in a dance. He lowered her gently down on to the bed, then unfastened his belt and slipped out of his dark trousers.

He stood there for a moment, in all his naked masculine glory, looking down at her. Then, slowly, he lowered himself down. Vanessa clung to him as his body covered hers, and then they were finally joined together, the pounding momentum building to a crescendo of pure soul-shattering pleasure.

Afterwards, they lay silently side by side for a long time, their passion spent, their breathing gradually returning to normal. Vanessa felt like a sleek, well-fed cat, purring after a satisfying meal. The long, hard body next to hers was turned slightly away, one arm flung over his head.

Finally she raised up on one elbow to lean over him. 'Rees?'

He opened one eye and glanced up at her. 'Hmm?' he murmured drowsily.

'What about the banquet?'

'Oh, bother the banquet.' He reached for her and pulled her down so that her head rested on his chest, the top of it tucked under his chin.

She pulled slightly away from him. 'I really do think we should put in an appearance,' she said.

He cocked one dark eyebrow at her. 'Really?'

She nodded. Then, suddenly aware of her nakedness, she jumped off the bed and ran over to retrieve her robe, which had earlier fallen on the floor.

She slipped it on, then went over to the cupboard and pulled out both the blue silk and the black crêpe dresses. When she turned back to him, he was standing beside the bed, just fastening the belt of his trousers.

'What do you think?' she asked, holding both dresses up.

He came closer, stood with his chin in his hand, inspecting the garments carefully, his eyes darting from one to the other. Finally, he pointed at the black crêpe.

'That one, I think.'

Her face fell. 'Really? I'm surprised.' She gave him a sly smile. 'I was positive you'd prefer the blue. It's far sexier.'

He nodded. 'Right. That's why I chose the black.' He reached out for her and gathered her to him, dresses and all. 'When you look sexy I want it to be just for me, not the whole convention.'

They barely made it in time for the last course of dinner, which was laid out in the large banquet room of the hotel on one long table, with the current leader of the association presiding at the head, surrounded by his minions.

'Well,' Rees murmured in her ear as they made their way to the two vacant chairs near the entrance. 'It looks as though we're just in time for the speeches.'

'Oh, goody,' she said drily. 'I just hope we'll get something to eat.'

They took their places as inconspicuously as possible. Thankfully they were near the entrance, so they didn't create quite as scandalous a spectacle as she'd feared, but, as Rees had predicted, the speeches began just then, and the attention of the audience was focused on the head of the table.

Although the meal that had already been set at their places was cold by the time they arrived, Vanessa was so hungry that she wolfed down the perennial chicken à la King, in all its congealed tasteless glory, as though it were the choicest gourmet dish, finishing up with a passable lemon pie.

She tried to concentrate on the speeches, but Rees's knee kept pressing against hers, so that even in the cool room she was flooded with warmth. Then, when his hand fell on her thigh, under the table-cloth, irresistible desire flared up in her. She knew she should brush the hand off, but she rather enjoyed the possessive gesture, and no one could see.

After the speeches there was dancing in the adjoining room, and then it was even harder for her to keep up a sedate appearance. The lights had been dimmed, and a small combo was playing—mainly old show tunes, with a sprinkling of more current music for the sparse contingent of younger guests. When he took her in his arms on the dance-floor, her body quite naturally moulded itself to his, and she was beyond caring what anyone thought.

With each step they took she could feel the heat and tension building between them until, finally, after fifteen minutes of it, he put his mouth next to her ear and murmured, 'Let's get out of here before I disgrace both of us right here on the dance-floor.'

She pulled her head back and looked up into his eyes, which were gleaming hotly with naked desire. She could only nod, and they made their way as unobtrusively but hastily as possible through the crowd.

The next morning, Vanessa awoke next to a man in her bed for the first time in her life. After leaving the banquet, he had quite naturally spent the night in her room, a night filled with wonderful lovemaking.

Watching him now as he slept, she went over the whole thing again in her mind, like a well-loved book, read and re-read. He had been so tender, so loving, so gentle with her, yet at the same time revealed an unbridled passion that made her feel utterly desirable.

But he hadn't spoken one word of love. Several times, at the height of her joy, she had almost blurted out her own love for him, but always stopped herself just in time, afraid it would spoil things. She kept telling herself it didn't matter, that his desire for her was enough, but her old fears wouldn't quite go away.

She slipped out of bed and went into the bathroom to shower. When she came back in her robe, a towel wrapped around her head, he was sitting up in bed, his head propped back against the pillows, watching her as she brushed out her damp hair.

'Today's our last day,' she said, coming back to sit beside him on the bed. 'Don't you think we should make it to at least one seminar? The last one is scheduled for ten o'clock, and our plane doesn't leave until late this afternoon.'

'No,' he said firmly. 'I don't.'

She gave him a look of mock severity. 'My, you're very casual about your employer. Don't you care about your job?'

'Not really,' he said with a grin. 'There are lots of jobs.' He reached out and slid a hand underneath the opening of her robe, fondling her breast. 'Right now, you're all that interests me. Come on,' he coaxed, placing his other hand at the back of her neck. 'Come back to bed.'

With a laugh, she slipped out of his arms and jumped to her feet. 'Rees, you're insatiable. All right, if you refuse to do your duty by Global Enterprises, I want to see something of Santa Barbara besides a hotel bedroom before we have to leave.'

He pulled the covers back and swung his legs over the side of the bed. 'I took you for a drive yesterday, woman,' he complained. 'What more do you want?'

She turned and walked away from him. 'Right now I'm starved and want some breakfast,' she said firmly. 'Then I'd like to take a walk on the beach. Now you go and get dressed.'

After a leisurely breakfast, they drove to the public beach just north of the small harbour. It was virtually deserted on a Sunday morning, the natives apparently all in church or in bed, the conventioneers at the seminar.

It was a sunny day, but balmy, not too hot, not too cool, with a slight breeze blowing off the ocean. They walked barefoot along the shore, hand in hand, until they came to small, secluded cove with a clump of palm trees screening it from the road.

'Shall we sit down?' Rees asked. They had brought along a large beach towel in case they wanted to swim. 'Or are you in the mood for a dip in the ocean?'

She'd worn a bathing-suit under her cotton shift, and Rees had on a short-sleeved white shirt over dark cotton trunks, his long legs bare. Vanessa ran the few feet down to the line of waves breaking against the shore, slipped out of one sandal and dipped her toe in the water as it rushed forward, foaming.

She shivered. 'No, I don't think so,' she called to him. 'It's too cold for me. How about you?'

He was spreading out the towel underneath a tree. 'No, thanks. My days of swimming in the ocean in February are long past. Come and sit down.'

'Ah,' she said as she came back to him. 'You were one of those California surfers we hear so much about.'

He laughed. 'Afraid so. It was part of growing up around here.'

He sat down on the towel, leaned his back against the trunk of the tree and held out a hand to her. She took his hand and knelt before him, facing him, a stern look on her face.

'If you have any ideas about making love to me on a public beach, Mr Malory, you can forget them.'

He raised innocent eyes. 'I had no such intention. I just want you close to me.'

She turned around and settled herself in front of him, leaning back against him. Immediately his arms came around her to hold her loosely from behind. She sighed happily and rested her head on his shoulder. They sat there for some time in silence, watching the waves as they broke on the shore, the small boats sailing in and out of the harbour, and listening to the roar of the surf, the caw of the gulls.

This must be what heaven is like, she thought happily, as she nestled against his broad chest. There was only one little nagging worry on her mind to mar the perfection of the day. What did the future hold in store for them? Did they even have a future? So far she had successfully brushed it away whenever it cropped up, reminding herself that she was already committed to whatever was ahead, that she would simply try to enjoy the present moment.

'Penny for them,' he said quietly at last.

She twisted her head around to smile up at him. 'Nothing very earth-shaking, I'm afraid. I think the tides have hypnotised me. It's all so perfect, Rees. I just hate to see it end.'

'Why does it have to end?' he said, tightening his grip on her waist. He kissed her lightly. 'Do you think God is going to strike you dead the minute you leave here?'

She laughed. 'Maybe something like that. I mean, I guess I've learned to mistrust happiness.'

'Are you happy, Vanessa?'

She nodded. 'Blissfully.' She hesitated a moment, then said, 'Are you?'

'You know I am. You do things to me I didn't think any woman could. And it's not just the physical part, great as that is. It's the whole package.' He chuckled. 'I think I was lost that first day I walked in the office and you said you'd drive the rig to Portland yourself if you couldn't find a driver. I knew then I wasn't going to let a woman like that get away from me.' Then suddenly he paused and his face clouded over.

'But I do have some unfinished business to take care of first.'

Vanessa sobered instantly and her imagination began to run riot. What unfinished business? Should she pin him down? 'Not a wife and children, lurking in the background, I hope,' she said lightly at last.

'Oh, lord, no,' he said with feeling. 'Nothing like that. Don't worry about it. Just trust me.'

She waited for him to go on, but instead he kissed her again, then leaned his head back and closed his eyes. She watched him for a moment, the well-loved features of his face etched in her mind: the long black lashes sweeping his high, prominent cheekbones, the fine, straight nose, the sensuous mouth, the strong chin.

Oh, I love you, Rees Malory, she whispered in her heart. I only pray you care about me half as much as I do about you.

That evening they flew back to Oregon and, with every mile, as reality came closer and closer, Vanessa's euphoria faded just a little more. But Rees *is* the reality, she told herself, glancing over at the man sitting beside her. Why can't I believe that?

After they'd picked up Rees's car at the small airport on the outskirts of town, the drive to her house was as silent as the plane ride. Ever since they left Santa Barbara, he'd seemed so preoccupied, so remote and distant, as though pondering some weighty matter. She longed to ask him what was troubling him, but decided in the end that she'd just have to be patient. He'd asked her to trust him, and she would.

She loved him; she knew he loved her. The future would work itself out.

When he dropped her at the house, he didn't kiss her, didn't even touch her, just said he'd see her in the morning at the office and drove off, almost, she thought, standing there as his car disappeared, as though he could hardly wait to get away from her.

Telling herself not to let her imagination run away with her, she let herself inside and set her bag down in the hall. She could hear the clatter of crockery coming from the kitchen, and when she got there Harriet was standing at the counter, her back to her, running water into the sink.

'Hi,' Vanessa called, coming up behind her. 'I'm home.'

Harriet turned around, a glad smile of welcome on her face. 'Oh, Vanessa!' She wiped her hands on her apron and crossed over to her. 'How was the convention?'

'Oh, all right,' was the offhand reply. 'Boring.'

Harriet cocked her head to one side and clucked her tongue. 'You don't look bored. In fact, you look positively radiant.'

Vanessa flushed. Trust Harriet to see beneath the surface at her first glance. She was certain, in fact, that her aunt had already formed a mental image of exactly what had gone on the entire weekend.

'Are you hungry, dear? I made a nice pot of vegetable soup for supper.'

'Sounds good. But let me get it. No need for you to wait on me.'

'Nonsense!' Harriet replied. 'I enjoy it. It'll only take a minute to heat. I made some corn bread, too, your favourite.'

'Well, if you insist. Guess I'll take my bags upstairs and wash. Just be a minute.'

She carried her suitcase up to her bedroom, took off the jacket to her suit, then went into the bathroom to wash. As she stood before the mirror, combing out her hair, she could see what Harriet meant by saying she looked radiant. Her eyes sparkled, her skin glowed, even her dark hair seemed to shine.

If that's what love does to one, she thought, as she made her way back downstairs, it's no wonder it's so hard to hide. Back in the kitchen she sat down at the table before a steaming bowl of soup. As she tucked in, Harriet settled down across from her with a cup of coffee.

'Now,' she said. 'Tell me all about it.'

'Well, as I said,' Vanessa commented between bites, 'it was pretty boring. But Santa Barbara is a lovely town, and the weather was perfect.'

Harriet waved a hand in the air. 'Oh, not about the convention or Santa Barbara, silly. I meant about Rees.'

Vanessa gave her aunt a warning look but, at the sight of those guileless grey eyes, so full of love and genuine interest, she didn't have the heart to deceive her. Besides, she longed to talk to someone about it, and, since Harriet had been promoting a romance between them from the day she'd first laid eyes on Rees Malory, who better to confide in?

'All right, Harriet,' she said with a sigh. 'Whatever it is you're thinking, you're probably right.'

'Aha!' Harriet exclaimed with satisfaction. 'So. You finally saw the light.' She leaned forward. 'Tell me what happened.'

And so, omitting the more intimate details, Vanessa proceeded to do just that. She told her about the trip to Lompoc to visit his sister, their walks on the beach, the things they had talked about, the banquet they'd attended, the dancing afterwards.

'It sounds as though you were inseparable,' Harriet commented when she'd finished.

Vanessa shrugged and smiled guiltily. 'Well, yes, I guess you could say that.'

Harriet rose and carried the dishes to the sink. 'Well, all I can say is that I'm delighted.' She came back with a cup of coffee for Vanessa and set it before her, standing there by her chair for a moment, looking down at her. 'I told you right from the beginning, didn't I, that he was quite a man?'

'Yes, Harriet,' she said with a smile. 'That you did.'

Harriet sat down and sipped for a moment on her fresh cup of coffee, then said, 'So, now what? I mean, have you made any plans?'

Vanessa frowned. 'Not really. Except to take things one day at a time.'

Harriet gave her a sharp look. 'Something's troubling you, I can tell.'

Vanessa decided to temporise. 'Oh, nothing really, except that I don't know how we're going to manage to work together after——' She reddened and broke

off as she realised the implications of what she'd
almost said.

'Oh, you're both so clever,' Harriet said airily. 'I'm
sure you'll find a way.' She was silent for a moment,
then said, 'But there's more to it than that, isn't there?
What is it?'

Vanessa turned her cup around slowly in its saucer,
staring down at it. 'I'm not quite sure.' She raised her
eyes. 'Even though he was more open with me than
before, really talked about his past life, there are still
so many gaps. I know he cares about me as much as
I do about him,' she added hastily. 'And I think his
intentions are—well, honourable, if you want to put
it that way—but now that the weekend is over, I can't
help thinking of all the things he didn't say.'

To her surprise, Harriet only nodded slowly. 'I can
see that,' she said at last. 'So I think you're right to
move cautiously, take it one step at a time. If he's let
you into his private life this far, he'll let you in all the
way in time.'

'Then you think I shouldn't push it? I mean, pin
him down?'

Harriet shook her head vigorously. 'No. Definitely
not. I think what matters here is whether you really
love him. Do you?'

'Yes,' Vanessa replied softly. 'Oh, yes, I do.'

'And he loves you?'

She hesitated. 'I believe he does, yes.'

'Then I don't see any problem.'

'No,' Vanessa said slowly. 'But then I loved David,
too, and thought he loved me.'

'Now, Vanessa, that's ancient history. You were a child then. You'll see. It'll all work itself out.' She got up from her chair. 'Now, my favourite programme comes on in five minutes, and I don't want to miss it.'

Vanessa smiled. Come hell or high water, wars, famines, the barbarians beating at the gates, Harriet wouldn't miss one of her television shows.

'I think I'll pass,' she said, getting up and carrying her cup to the sink. 'I need a bath and then early to bed. Tomorrow's a working day.'

She started to leave, but when she reached the door heard Harriet call after her and turned around.

'I almost forgot,' her aunt said. 'Robert's back in town and has been calling you. Seems his case in Denver is finally over.'

Robert! She'd forgotten completely about him. Immediately she felt guilty about it. But she'd never promised Robert anything. All the caring had been on his side. She valued his friendship, but had never led him to believe there could be anything more between them. Still, she'd have to tell him about Rees eventually.

'Well, I guess I'd better call him,' she said.

'Yes, dear, I really think you'd better.'

She went into the den to use the telephone there and dialled his number. As she waited for him to answer, she tried to decide just how much to tell him. Probably nothing right now, she finally decided. At least not until she had something definite to say.

Then his voice came on the line. 'Hello.'

'Hello, Robert. This is Vanessa. Harriet said you called.'

'Yes. We finally finished up in Denver, and I'm back in town, for good I hope. How was the convention?'

'Boring,' she said truthfully. 'You know how those things are. Mediocre meals and dull speeches.'

'Did you make any useful contacts?'

'Not really. I'm not even sure why Global wanted me to go. But since they call all the shots now, I just do what I'm told.'

'Actually, that's the main reason I called,' he said. 'Since I've been back I've done some digging about your Mr Malory.'

Vanessa's ears perked up. 'Yes?' she said. 'And what did you find out?'

'Well, it seems he's a real dark horse. As it turns out, he's part-owner of the company.'

Vanessa sank down in the chair beside the telephone and drew in a sharp breath. 'The company?' she finally managed to croak out. 'You mean Global Enterprises?'

'Yes. Seems it started out as a family business, you know, founded by his grandfather, then run by his father and a series of uncles. Apparently Rees is the last Malory, and although the company went public some time ago he still owns the majority of the stock.'

By now Vanessa didn't even hear what he was saying. All she could think of was that Rees had lied to her, deceived her, right from the beginning. He had come as a spy, just as she'd feared.

'Robert, are you sure?' she said when she could speak.

'Oh, quite sure. I really had to hunt, do some clever detective work, but it's all there in black and white.' He read, ' "Rees Malory, vice-president in charge of operations." That's just a convenient way of disguising his real importance. So,' he went on, 'it looks as though you had his number right from the beginning. He obviously came here to check up on you, just as you suspected.' He laughed. 'Hope you've behaved yourself.'

Behaved herself! She'd made an utter fool of herself! Treating him as an employee—a *trainee*, for heaven's sake—when all along he owned her company.

'Well, thanks, Robert,' she said faintly at last, hoping he wouldn't notice the tremor in her voice. 'You've been a big help.'

After they hung up she sat there for several moments with her hand still on the receiver, simply staring blankly into space. From another part of the house came the distant sound of Harriet's television programme, muted laughter, applause, music.

She shook herself and slowly rose to her feet. Then she went over to the drinks cupboard and poured herself a glass of sherry—anything to clear her head of this dull, oppressive weight on it. As she sipped the fiery liquid, her one thought was—I never learn. I've done it again. Let some dashing man sweep me off my feet and blind me to what I knew was there all the time.

She drained her glass and carried it into the kitchen. While she was at the sink rinsing it out, to her dismay she heard her aunt coming down the hall, chuckling to herself over her programme. It was too late to escape her now. She turned around and waited.

As Harriet came inside she had already started to tell Vanessa the joke, but the minute she saw the look on her face she stopped in mid-sentence and stood there, staring. 'Child,' she said at last, crossing over to her. 'What in the world has happened? You look as though you've seen a ghost.'

Vanessa smiled wanly. 'I think possibly I have.' It was then she started to shake, a violent tremor that made her knees buckle.

Quickly Harriet's arm came around her, drawing her closely up against her plump waist. 'Come on, darling,' she soothed. 'Tell Auntie all about it.'

That was all it took. The tears that had been hovering behind her eyes from the moment she'd heard Robert's dreadful news now spilled over. She covered her face with her hands as the great sobs racked her body, heaving and gasping. Harriet just stood beside her, holding her, patting her shoulder rhythmically and saying, 'There, there,' until the spasm passed.

Then she reached for the box of tissues on the draining-board, took one out and handed it to Vanessa. She took it, wiped her eyes and blew her nose loudly, then opened the lower cupboard door and threw the sodden tissue in the rubbish bin.

'I'm sorry, Harriet,' she said shakily. She shook her head. 'I just couldn't help it.'

'Come and sit down,' Harriet said, taking her hand and leading her over to the table. 'And tell me all about it.'

It was too late to hedge at this point. Harriet had
seen the worst, and no harm could be done now by
telling her the whole sordid story. Still, she couldn't
quite seem to form the words on her tongue. Every
time she tried, her voice would start to waver and the
tears threatened once again.

Finally, Harriet sighed. 'There's only one thing I
can think of that would upset you this badly. It's got
to be Rees.'

Dumbly, Vanessa nodded, but still couldn't speak.

'He's married,' Harriet said flatly. Vanessa shook
her head. 'Engaged?' Another shake. Harriet
frowned. 'Is he an escaped criminal? Gay?'

By now, Vanessa had to smile at her aunt's wild
speculations. She got up to get another tissue from
the box on the counter, blew her nose more
thoroughly, then came back to sit down. The small
activity, and Harriet's calm presence, had settled her
down to the point where she could at least talk about
it now.

She cleared her throat. 'I just talked to Robert,' she
said. 'I had asked him some time ago to look into
Rees's position in the company. Now he's discovered
that instead of the trainee I was led to believe he was,
he's actually the owner of the company. At least, the
major stockholder.'

Harriet's mouth flew open and her eyes widened.
'Well, land's sake!' she said at last. Then she smiled
smugly. 'I knew he had to be something special, a lot
more than he let on. So, he's a real tycoon. What do
they call it? Chief executive officer. My, isn't that im-

pressive?' She gave Vanessa a bewildered look. 'But why are you crying about that?'

'Harriet!' Vanessa exploded. 'He lied to me! He deceived me! Right from the beginning.'

Harriet almost jumped out of her chair at the heated outburst. 'Well, yes,' she said slowly. 'I suppose you could look at it that way.'

'How else is there to look at it?' she cried. She got up and started pacing around the floor, wringing her hands and groaning. 'What's more,' she went on heatedly, 'he had to be the one who arranged that whole weekend in Santa Barbara.' Even the connecting rooms, she added silently.

'Now, dear,' Harriet was saying, 'I really think you're making too much out of this. I mean, there's nothing wrong with a man trying to protect his investment.' She smiled. 'And if you're right about the weekend, don't you think it's rather flattering?'

'No!' Vanessa cried, coming to stand before her. 'I don't. All he ever wanted was to take over Farnham's, to ease me out.'

'Now, why would he want to do that?'

'Just because all a man like that cares about is winning. Power. Control. Besides, a lie is a lie. If he deceived me about his real position in Global, he's probably deceived me about everything else.' She groaned again. 'Will I never learn? He was so much like David. I should have known.'

'I don't really see that there's much similarity between them,' Harriet commented mildly. 'Rees may have fudged a little on his true identity, but I don't think he had any ulterior motive. He probably just wanted to see how you handled the business without your trying to impress him.' She shook her head firmly. 'No, dear, he's nothing like David.'

'Oh, Harriet, they could be twins! You don't know him. The same sweet-talk, the same arrogance...' She turned away. 'There's no way I can make you understand. I just feel so manipulated, so—so *used*!'

With a sigh, Harriet got up from her chair and came over to give her a hug. 'Why don't you go have your bath now? I'll make you a nice cup of cocoa, and after a good night's sleep you'll feel better in the morning.'

Vanessa gazed blankly at her. If only it were that simple. In the morning she'd have to face him!

CHAPTER NINE

AFTER a sleepless night, the next morning Vanessa's grief and shock had turned into a cold, hard anger. She skipped breakfast and left early, mainly to avoid Harriet, but also hoping to catch Rees before Sandra showed up.

When she arrived at the car park, she was gratified to see the grey rental Peugeot in its usual parking space. She got out, slammed her car door shut and marched directly to the office, her jaw set, her eyes straight ahead, determined to get this over with as quickly as possible.

He could have the company! It was what he came for. Learning the business! Sure, so he could ease her out and assume total control himself. And part of his strategy was to sweet-talk her into bed, to disarm her, lull her suspicions. It would make his take-over, when it came, that much simpler.

Through the window she saw him, standing at the filing cabinet, his back towards her. Snooping again, no doubt. When she came inside, he turned around, a pleased smile spreading across his face, and came walking towards her.

'Good morning,' he said softly. 'Sleep well?'

He put a hand out, but before he could touch her she backed away, out of his reach. She marched over to her desk, slammed her bag down on top, then turned to face him, her arms crossed in front of her, breathing fire.

Then, when she saw the puzzled expression on his face, she faltered for a moment, weakening. She had been in love with this man, trusted him, believed him, given herself to him. As the shame of that memory swept over her, her resolve hardened once again.

'I spoke to Robert last night,' she said in a clipped voice. 'He had some very interesting information for me.'

His eyes were wary now, watchful. 'Oh? What about?'

'About you. About your true position in Global Enterprises.'

He gave her one startled look, then his face closed down. He put his hands in his trouser pockets, turned away from her and walked slowly over to his desk. He leaned his hips back against it, his long legs stretched out in front of him.

'I see,' he said at last in a low voice. 'Look, Vanessa, I'm sorry you had to find out that way. I intended to tell you myself, as soon as I could think of a way to do it so you'd understand.'

She laughed harshly. 'Your "unfinished business", I suppose.' He nodded bleakly, and she went on. 'Well, now you don't have to, do you? You've won without firing a shot. You've not only got control of Farnham's, but you managed to do it by making a fool of me.'

He pushed himself away from the desk. 'No!' he said explosively. 'It's not like that.'

She narrowed her eyes at him. 'You deceived me, Rees. You lied to me.'

'All right,' he said. 'I admit I came here under false pretences. At the time it seemed like a good idea. We'd just acquired your company. Someone had to check it out, make sure it was going to be run properly. We'd invested rather heavily in it, and had that right. I volunteered mainly because it would bring me closer to California and I could visit Susan more often.'

'I don't believe you,' she said flatly. 'You came here to spy on me, to take over, to ease me out.'

'Oh, Vanessa, don't be childish! I could have done that any time I wanted. I'm telling you the truth. I just had to make sure our investment was secure.'

'Then why the great seduction? Is it just that you have to have every woman you meet? Is your ego really that fragile? I mean, it's obvious to me now that you were the one who arranged the weekend in Santa Barbara.' She raised an eyebrow. 'Even the convenient connecting rooms, I imagine.'

'All right,' he said. 'I admit that, too. I wanted you; I believed you were attracted to me. But to pursue a more personal relationship I had to get you away from this damned office.'

She drew herself up to her full height. 'This "damned office" happens to be my life!'

'Well, if that's really true, I pity you.'

They stood there for several long moments, their eyes locked together, neither giving an inch. Finally, Rees waved a hand in the air and came to stand before her.

'Listen, Vanessa,' he said softly. 'The weekend was wonderful, you know it was. You're not going to let a minor detail like this spoil things for us, are you?'

'Minor detail! It's been one long deception from the day you walked into this office.' She shook her head angrily. 'Well, you got everything you wanted. It just makes me sick and ashamed to think I fell for it. I trusted you, believed in you.' She gave him a withering look. 'But I've been through that before and lived, so I guess I can do it again.'

He put his face close to hers, glowering darkly. 'You want to know what I think?' he snarled.

'Not especially.'

'Well, I'm going to tell you anyway. I think your paranoia about men is at the bottom of this whole thing.'

She cocked an eyebrow at him. 'Oh, really? Well, if that's true, just remember that it's men like you who made me that way.'

She couldn't stand another moment in his presence. She picked up her bag, marched to the door, then whirled around when she reached it. 'You got my company and you made me fall in love with you. Now you can do what you want. I just never want to see you again.'

She drove around aimlessly for what seemed like hours. She couldn't go home—she'd have to face Harriet—and she couldn't go back to the office. It wasn't until she was getting so low on fuel that she was afraid she'd run out if she didn't fill the tank soon that she headed slowly back to town.

As she passed the office, she saw that Rees's car
was gone from the car park. Her anger still
smouldered, but beneath it lurked a deep sense of grief
and loss that she knew she'd have to deal with
eventually. And now she wouldn't even have her work.
If Rees's company hadn't already gobbled up
Farnham's before, they surely would now, after the
things she'd said to him.

She glanced at her watch. It was past noon. Sandra
would be out to lunch, perhaps Rees, too. On an impulse, she swung into the car park.

The door to the office was locked, and when she
let herself in there was no one inside. As she glanced
around the familiar, cluttered room, possibly for the
last time, she noticed that Rees's desk had been cleared
completely and that the files he'd been working on
were neatly stacked on her own desk. There were notes
in his slashing black handwriting pinned to them as
to their status. She made a hurried search of his desk
drawers, but there was nothing in them to indicate
he'd ever occupied it, not a trace of him.

Obviously he'd left—probably for good, from all
indications—and, although she knew it had to be, she
couldn't quite dismiss a pang of real regret. Nor did
she want to be there in case he did return.

She locked up the office again, ran back to her car
and headed home.

'What are you doing home at this hour?' Harriet
called to her from the den.

'Oh, I think I'm coming down with a bug,' she
called back, and headed for the stairs, hoping to avoid

a confrontation. Since her head was now pounding unbearably, it wasn't exactly a lie.

But before she'd gone halfway, Harriet appeared in the hallway, peering up at her. 'What kind of bug? Should I call the doctor?'

'No, it's nothing serious,' she replied, forcing out a smile. 'Just a general achiness. I'll be all right once I lie down.'

'Can I get you something? Don't you want some lunch?'

'The thought of food made her gag. 'No, thanks. Don't worry about me. I'm going to try to get some sleep. I'll be fine.'

'Well, if you're sure. And where have you been? Rees has been calling all morning.'

Vanessa's face hardened. 'I don't want to talk to Rees Malory. Not ever again.'

Before Harriet could argue with her, she turned and ran swiftly to her room. By now the top of her head felt as though it were coming off. After a trip to the bathroom for aspirin, she stripped off her trousers and shirt, and put on a warm robe, then lay down on top of the bed and closed her eyes.

Immediately, visions of Rees and their weekend together rose up in her mind to torment her. Eventually, however, the aspirin and sheer exhaustion did their work, and she drifted into a fitful sleep.

When she awoke, it was already growing dark outside. She turned on the lamp beside the bed, blinked, then glanced at her watch. It was six o'clock. She'd slept for five hours. She dragged herself out of bed and went into the bathroom.

When she came back she heard a light tapping on the door. All she needed was Harriet hovering over her. With a resigned sigh, she hopped back into bed, pulled the covers up, and called, 'Come in.'

The door swung open, and Harriet came inside, carrying a tray containing a steaming bowl of soup and a plate of crackers. 'I thought you might be able to eat something by now,' she said, setting the tray down on the bedside table. 'Good old chicken soup. It'll cure anything.'

'Thanks, Harriet,' she said, sitting up. 'It smells good.'

'Oh, and Rees just called again. I told him you were sick in bed and that I'd have you call him back when you felt better.'

Vanessa glared at her. 'If he calls again, tell him I'm dead,' she said grimly.

'Now, dear, don't do anything you'll be sorry for. Just last night, remember, you seemed to be very much in love with him.'

Vanessa waved a hand in the air. 'That was last night. Today all that has changed.'

'Vanessa, you don't mean to tell me you've broken things off with him just because——?'

'Because he lied to me? Yes, of course I have. And Harriet,' she added in a warning tone, 'I really and truly do not want to discuss it. I mean it.'

Harriet stared at her for several long moments. Then she shook her head slowly and her round face took on a mournful expression. 'All right,' she said at last. 'Have it your way. I won't say another word.'

As the days passed, with no word from Global about her position as manager of Farnham's, Vanessa's fears began to abate. After all, she did a good job for them. Why had she been so afraid that they'd try to get rid of her? It would have been bad business practice.

After that last day, Rees had never shown up at the office again, and poor Sandra was totally bewildered by his abrupt disappearance. She kept harping on the subject until Vanessa thought she'd scream if she heard his name one more time. Finally, one day, a few weeks after he'd left, she exploded.

'Sandra, the man is gone! Can't you understand? He's not coming back.'

'But I still miss him. He was so nice.' Her voice took on a whining tone. 'And he didn't even say goodbye.'

Vanessa silently ground her back teeth together. Nice! If Sandra only knew. 'No,' Vanessa snapped. 'He didn't. Now would you please quit talking about him? I'm sick to death of hearing his name every five minutes.'

Sandra's lip quivered. 'Well, I'm sorry. You don't need to shout at me.'

Vanessa shut her eyes, fighting for control. 'I'm sorry, Sandra,' she said at last. 'I didn't mean to shout at you. Now, please, let's forget about Rees Malory and try to get some work done around here.'

*   *   *

During those weeks she somehow dragged herself through the long days and nights, trying desperately to keep all thoughts of Rees out of her mind and heart. She was grateful that at least she still had her job. It was the only thing that kept her sane, but even that had lost its zest for her.

True to her word, Harriet never mentioned his name again, but Vanessa was uncomfortably aware of the reproachful looks darted her way from time to time, just as though *she* were the one in the wrong, and, from the way her aunt tiptoed around the house, one would think there'd been a death in the family.

Well, someone—or something—had died, she thought glumly one night at dinner. What was worse, as time passed and she still heard nothing from Global, the awful suspicion began to form in her mind that maybe Harriet was right: that perhaps she *had* been wrong to dismiss him so quickly, refusing to hear his side, even to discuss it with him.

As her conviction of her own fault in the matter grew, her pain became even more unbearable. It was one thing to feel like the victim of a diabolical plot, but quite another to suspect the actual break-up was entirely her own fault. She'd been so sure at the time that he'd only used her. Now she wasn't so sure. Maybe he'd been right in blaming her own paranoia.

That night she sat at the table, her head propped on one hand, her elbow braced on the table, staring into space and pushing her food around on her plate with her fork.

'Vanessa!' Harriet said sharply. Startled, she raised her head and blinked at her aunt. 'Vanessa,' she re-

peated more gently. 'I know I promised not to mention
Rees again, but I simply can't bear to watch you eating
your heart out this way. Look at you. You're a mess.
You just mope around the house, you're working too
hard, you've lost weight, you've put away all your
lovely new clothes, let your appearance go to seed.'
She stopped suddenly, out of breath.

Vanessa sat up a little straighter and made a stab
at a smile. 'Well, thanks a lot, Harriet. That really
helps my morale.'

'Well, I'm sorry, but the time has come when you
need to hear a few home truths. You're going to listen
to me whether you like it or not.'

'Oh, Harriet,' she said wearily. 'I know what you're
going to say and, to tell you the honest truth, the main
reason I don't want to hear it is because I'm afraid
you might be right.'

Harriet's mild grey eyes widened in disbelief. 'You
are?'

Vanessa nodded. 'Yes, but it doesn't matter. It's
too late now.'

'No, it's not,' Harriet rejoined tartly. 'If you really
love him, isn't he worth fighting for?'

'There's nothing I can do, don't you see?' Tears
stung behind her eyes. 'I've blown it. Me and my
stupid pride.'

'You could go to him, call him, try to contact him.'

Vanessa shook her head. 'Not after the things I said
to him that last day.' She got up from the table. 'Let's
just forget it, OK? How about if I watch your programme with you?'

*   *   *

A few nights later, just as Vanessa was coming in the door after work, the telephone started to ring. Since Harriet's car wasn't in the driveway, she obviously wasn't home, so she ran into the den to answer it herself.

'Vanessa?' came a woman's voice. 'Vanessa Farnham?'

'Yes, this is she.' The voice sounded vaguely familiar, but she couldn't quite place it.

'This is Susan Malory, Rees's sister. If you remember, we met several weeks ago when you and he came to visit me.'

'Of course I remember, Susan. How are you?'

'Doing much better, I'm happy to say. In fact, the doctors think I might be able to get out of the wheelchair soon.'

'That's wonderful, Susan. I'm so glad.'

There was a short pause, and Vanessa stood there, holding the telephone, waiting, wondering why on earth Susan had called her.

Finally the girl laughed nervously. 'Actually, the main reason I called was to ask you what you've done to my brother. Not that it's any of my business,' she added hurriedly. 'But he's been in such a black mood for the past several weekends that I was getting really worried about him. I thought he might be sick and wasn't telling me. Then, finally, I asked him about you and he almost took the top of my head off. And that's not like him.'

Vanessa didn't know what to say. All she could think of was that Rees was hurting too, to the point, it seemed, where his sister was so concerned that she'd

taken it upon herself to call and question her about
it. A great weight seemed to be slowly lifting from
her heart and her spirits began to soar.

'Anyway,' Susan was going on, 'I finally decided
to do something about it. I mean, it's possible you
don't care anything about him, but when you were
here it seemed so obvious to me that you were both
very much in love that I couldn't just stand by and
do nothing.' She paused. 'I hope you're not furious
at me.'

'No,' Vanessa said. 'I'm not furious. Not at all. In
fact, I'm very grateful. But I'm afraid you're too late.
Our last meeting was pretty sticky. In fact, I treated
Rees rather badly, and I don't think there's anything
I can do about it now.'

'Can I make a suggestion?'

'Sure. Anything.'

'Why don't you fly down this weekend to visit me?'

Vanessa was stunned. She couldn't do that. Could
she? But why not? What did she have to lose? All he
could do was send her away, and Harriet had been
right again. If she loved him he was worth fighting
for.

'All right,' she said at last. 'I think I'll do just that.'

That Saturday morning she flew to Santa Barbara.
At the airport she rented a car and drove up the coast
to Lompoc. She had no plans, no idea where she'd
stay that night, or even *if* she'd stay. All she knew
was that she had to see him. What happened afterwards didn't bear speculation.

At the nursing home, as she drove through the iron gates, her heart began to pound so hard that she felt it would jump out of her chest. Would Rees even be there? What would she say to him if he was?

She parked in front of the low stucco building, then got out and stood there, still shaky, looking around and wondering how to find Susan. It was just past noon. She decided to go inside and ask for Susan at the desk, but as she started to walk towards the entrance she saw them just coming outside, not ten feet away.

At the same moment, Rees's eyes fell on her. He did a double take, blinked in the bright sunshine, then stood stock-still, staring at her, the frown deepening on his face, not uttering a word.

Vanessa shook herself and started walking slowly towards them, her heart still thudding in her ears, her eyes fastened on the tall man. Just the sight of him warmed her heart, but as she came closer she could see that Susan was right. The green eyes had lost their sparkle, his face was gaunt and haggard, and he looked as though he hadn't slept for days.

'Oh, Vanessa,' Susan cried, wheeling towards her. 'You did come. How wonderful to see you again.' She turned to her brother. 'Don't just stand there, Rees. Come and say hello to Vanessa. I think I'll go inside and get my sweater. It's a little chillier than I thought.' She winked at Vanessa, then turned her chair around and made straight back for the entrance, passing Rees on the way without a glance.

'Hello, Rees,' Vanessa said.

'Vanessa,' he said flatly. 'What are you doing here?'

'Your sister invited me,' she replied. 'And I felt I needed a few days off.'

'And who's running your precious business?' His tone was not quite sneering, but there was a definite note of sarcasm in it.

She shrugged. 'It'll have to run itself for a few days.' She looked up directly into his eyes, which were as hard and cold as green marble. 'I had more important things on my mind.'

'Such as?'

This was turning out to be much harder than she'd imagined. What did he want her to do? Throw herself at his feet? Humble herself even more? Or possibly, at this point, just get lost? It had been a mistake to come. He obviously didn't want her. And she couldn't really blame him after the way she'd treated him.

'Nothing, I guess,' she mumbled at last. 'In fact, I can see I shouldn't have come. I can visit Susan another time.'

She turned and started moving away from him, but before she'd taken a step she felt his hand on her arm, holding her back. She stopped, every muscle tense, her heart in her throat, waiting to see what he'd do. He put his other hand on her shoulder and turned her around slowly to face him.

'What I should do is beat you,' he said sternly.

She shrugged. 'I guess I couldn't blame you.'

Then his mouth twitched a little at the edges and he almost smiled. 'Come on, let's take a walk around the grounds. I think we need to talk.'

They set off down the curving driveway and soon came to a narrow, paved pathway that meandered across the wide green lawn. Beyond it was a woody area, where three or four smaller stucco buildings nestled among the trees. The path was bordered by bright flower-beds, and white wooden benches were placed at various intervals along the way. When they came to one that was unoccupied, he turned to her.

'Let's sit down for a few minutes, shall we?'

She nodded. 'All right.'

They sat there side by side for some time without speaking, Vanessa tense and still, Rees leaning forward, his elbows braced on his knees, his head in his hands, staring into the distance. Watching him covertly, Vanessa was struck anew by the sheer animal magnetism of the man. Memories of their weekend together flooded into her mind, and she longed to reach out, just to touch him.

After the first cold reaction to her presence there, he seemed to have thawed a little, but she still sensed a distance between them that she couldn't quite breach. If only he'd say something! Finally, the silence became unbearable. She cleared her throat and turned to him.

'I thought about writing to you, but didn't know where you were. Still living out of hotels, I suppose.'

'For the moment,' he replied. He turned to her. 'Actually I'm in the process of negotiating for a house in Santa Barbara.'

'What? I can hardly believe that, a rolling stone like you.'

He shrugged. 'I thought it might be time I settled down.'

'What about your work? The Global head office is in New York, isn't it?'

'That doesn't matter. I never really took part in the day-to-day running of the company anyway. There's a very competent staff to do that. All I need to do there is attend an occasional board of directors meeting, just to keep my oar in. Besides, New York isn't the end of the world in this age of jet travel.'

There was another long silence, and finally she decided to try again. 'Susan looks well,' she said. 'She tells me the doctors say she might be able to get out of the wheelchair soon. I——'

'Damn it,' he broke in angrily, turning on her and glaring. 'Why did you really come?'

She was about to hedge again, to repeat that she'd come to see Susan, but something in his eyes stopped her. Why lie at this point? She had come to try to mend fences with him. It was probably her last chance. Why not just tell him so?

She took a deep breath. 'All right. I came to see you. When she called me, Susan said—no, she implied—you'd probably be here this weekend.'

'Why?' he asked evenly. 'Hadn't you already said enough the last time?'

She flushed deeply. 'Well, I wanted to apologise for that. I mean, even though you did mislead me about your position in the company, I was wrong not to listen to you. At the time all I could think of was that you'd used me—you know, in our personal relations—and I just saw red.'

'I never deceived you about that,' he said slowly. 'What would I have had to gain? Didn't it ever occur to you that if I really wanted control of Farnham's I could have just taken it? It's part of my job to check out all our new acquisitions, to learn about their operations firsthand, and we'd never owned a trucking company before. I told you the truth. I came to learn.'

'Why couldn't you have told me that right from the beginning?'

'Because I've learned that the minute people find out who I really am, they either put on a show for me and hide all the little—and sometimes big—flaws in their operations, or they get suspicious and imagine I've come to take over.'

'Like me.'

He nodded. 'Just like you.' He reached over and took her hand. 'I never wanted your business, Vanessa,' he said softly. 'I wanted you.'

She eyed him carefully. 'Well, you got that, didn't you? As a matter of fact, if you'd told me the truth yourself that weekend in Santa Barbara, by then it wouldn't have made any difference. I went into it with my eyes open, and I was already committed.' She smiled. 'I may be paranoid, but I'm not stupid.' Then the smile faded. 'What hurt was having to hear it from Robert.'

His hand tightened on hers, and he moved closer to her, so that their bodies were touching. 'I know that now,' he said in a low voice. 'But by then I was so afraid of losing you I didn't know what to do, how to handle it.' He shrugged. 'What started out to be a pleasant affair ended up with my falling in love for the first time in my life, and I simply panicked.'

Vanessa could only stare at him, hardly able to believe her ears. Here was a man who had it all—looks, money, a captain of industry—in a panic over losing her! It struck her then just how much power she wielded over him, and with that knowledge came the confidence to make herself vulnerable to him.

She put a hand on his face and looked directly into his eyes. 'Didn't you know, Rees, how deeply I'd fallen in love with you? How could you have missed it?'

The green eyes gleamed emerald fire. 'I haven't had that much experience with love,' he said gruffly, his voice hoarse with emotion.

He covered the hand on his cheek with his, then turned it over and pressed his lips on the palm. A great warmth had begun to steal through Vanessa's whole body, a burning desire that filled her mind, heart and soul. It was going to be all right. Rees loved her!

Just then, out of the corner of her eye, she saw a group of people coming towards them down the path, laughing and talking. Rees turned around at the sound, then rose quickly to his feet, still holding her hand in his.

'Come on,' he said. 'Let's get out of here.'

'Where?' she asked, getting up and following along with him as he strode away towards the wooded copse.

'I'm staying in one of the guest cottages,' he said, pointing straight ahead. 'Over there, just beyond the trees.'

It was only a short walk. When they arrived, Rees unlocked the door, and they stepped inside a small sitting-room, which was cool and dim from the shade of the overhanging branches, sparsely furnished, but comfortable.

The minute they were inside, he kicked the door shut behind him, and reached out for her. She fell into his arms, and they stood there, motionless, for several heavenly moments. It felt so right to be here, safe at last in the arms of the man she loved, and as she heaved a deep sigh of sheer contentment his hand began to move rhythmically on her back, over the thin material of her cotton sun-dress. He dipped his head to nuzzle his mouth softly along her neck, and the irresistible warmth spread through her again.

Then he raised his head and, with his arms still enfolding her closely, looked down into her eyes. Forgive me, darling?' he murmured.

'There's nothing to forgive,' she whispered.

With a groan, his mouth came down on hers, hard and demanding at first, drawing in her lips, then gently, coaxingly, forcing them open. She flung her arms around his neck and pressed herself against him, aching to feel the hard, muscular body along its full length next to hers.

She raked her fingers through his thick dark hair, every nerve in her body aflame, responding to him without reservation. His hands were on her shoulders now, and he tore his mouth away to look down at her again, his eyes hooded, gleaming with desire. Slowly, his gaze never leaving hers, his hands slid down her body, lingering over her straining breasts, then fumbling with the buttons of her dress.

'I want to see you, Vanessa,' he rasped thickly.

She drew in her breath sharply and nodded, then stood before him, quite still as he slowly, carefully finished unfastening the dress and slipped it over her shoulders. His hands came back to pull down the straps of her slip, until both garments fell to the floor.

Her bare skin burned under his hungry gaze, and she lifted her chin slightly to mask the sudden shyness. His hands reached out to cover her breasts, the strong tapering fingers moulding the soft fullness, and she moaned deep in her throat as his thumbs began circling around the taut peaks.

Then, almost in a frenzy, she reached out to tug his white knit shirt up, until his smooth chest was bare. When he'd pulled it over his head, tousling the dark hair, she bent down to touch the warm bare skin of his chest with her lips. She could feel the rapid beating of his heart, the muscles quivering under her mouth as it moved over his body.

He pulled her into his arms again, crushing her breasts against his bare chest. 'Let's go into the bedroom, darling,' he murmured at her ear.

She nodded, and they walked together, still closely entwined, down a short hallway to a small dark room with a narrow white bed in the centre. At the side of the bed he turned to her, looking down into her eyes.

'I love you, Vanessa,' he said. 'And I want you more than I've ever wanted anything in my life.'

'I want you, too, Rees,' she breathed. 'And you know I love you.'

She hesitated for a second then, daringly, her fingers began to fumble at the buckle of his belt. His hands dropped to his sides and he stood rigid, looking down at her, as she pulled the dark trousers down over his lean hips and long legs.

When he stepped out of the trousers, she ran her hands back up slowly along the muscled legs, covered with coarse dark hair, over the flat, hard stomach, until once again her arms twined around his neck, and she arched her body up closely to his, joyously aware of his hard, aching need of her.

As his arms came around her again, and his lips claimed hers, his tongue thrusting, probing the soft interior of her mouth, they sank slowly down on to the bed. As they came together at last, Vanessa gave herself to him totally, meeting his pulsing need with wild abandon, secure now in the knowledge that he loved her completely.

She dozed for a while, and when she awoke she found him propped up on one elbow, gazing down at her.

'You're not leaving now,' he said sternly, the moment her eyes fluttered open. 'You're going to stay here with me.'

She laughed. 'Rees, we can't stay here together, not in the guest-house.'

'Well, as it happens, I have a room in our hotel in Santa Barbara.'

'Connecting rooms?' she asked with a twinkle in her eye.

He shook his head. 'No. And since there's another convention going on I doubt if you'll be able to get a room of your own. We just may have to share.' He gave her a sideways glance. 'Although,' he added, shifting gears, 'if you still don't trust me, we can always get married first. Of course, I understand there's a three-day waiting period in California.'

'Oh? Sounds as if you've looked into it.'

He only smiled enigmatically and reached out for her.

But she had already moved deftly out of his grasp. 'And what about my business?' she asked.

He waved a hand in the air. 'We can work out those details later on. I like Oregon. We can live there if you want. The important thing is that we be together, always.' He reached for her again. 'Now, quit talking and come here.'

This time she fell happily into his arms and, as she nestled there against his broad bare shoulder, it struck her forcibly that learning to love meant trusting even when you weren't sure, even making yourself so vulnerable to another person that you risked getting badly hurt.

On the other hand, it was well worth the risk, since she also knew now that a life without love was no life at all.

Accept 4 FREE Romances and 2 FREE gifts

FROM READER SERVICE

An irresistible invitation from Mills & Boon Reader Service. Please accept our offer of 4 free Romances, a CUDDLY TEDDY and a special MYSTERY GIFT... Then, if you choose, go on to enjoy 6 captivating Romances every month for just £1.70 each, postage and packing free. Plus our FREE Newsletter with author news, competitions and much more.

Send the coupon below to:
Reader Service, FREEPOST,
PO Box 236, Croydon,
Surrey CR9 9EL.

NO STAMP REQUIRED

Yes! Please rush me 4 Free Romances and 2 free gifts!
Please also reserve me a Reader Service Subscription. If I decide to subscribe I can look forward to receiving 6 brand new Romances each month for just £10.20, post and packing free.
If I choose not to subscribe I shall write to you within 10 days - I can keep the books and gifts whatever I decide. I may cancel or suspend my subscription at any time. I am over 18 years of age.

Ms/Mrs/Miss/Mr ———————————————————— EP30R

Address ————————————————————————

————————————————————————————————

Postcode——————————Signature ——————————

Next Month's Romances

Each month you can choose from a wide variety of romance with Mills & Boon. Below are the new titles to look out for next month, why not ask either Mills & Boon Reader Service or your Newsagent to reserve you a copy of the titles you want to buy — just tick the titles you would like and either post to Reader Service or take it to any Newsagent and ask them to order your books.

Please save me the following titles:	Please tick	✓
HIGH RISK	Emma Darcy	
PAGAN SURRENDER	Robyn Donald	
YESTERDAY'S ECHOES	Penny Jordan	
PASSIONATE CAPTIVITY	Patricia Wilson	
LOVE OF MY HEART	Emma Richmond	
RELATIVE VALUES	Jessica Steele	
TRAIL OF LOVE	Amanda Browning	
THE SPANISH CONNECTION	Kay Thorpe	
SOMETHING MISSING	Kate Walker	
SOUTHERN PASSIONS	Sara Wood	
FORGIVE AND FORGET	Elizabeth Barnes	
YESTERDAY'S DREAMS	Margaret Mayo	
STORM OF PASSION	Jenny Cartwright	
MIDNIGHT STRANGER	Jessica Marchant	
WILDER'S WILDERNESS	Miriam Macgregor	
ONLY TWO CAN SHARE	Annabel Murray	

If you would like to order these books in addition to your regular subscription from Mills & Boon Reader Service please send £1.80 per title to: Mills & Boon Reader Service, Freepost, P.O. Box 236, Croydon, Surrey, CR9 9EL, quote your Subscriber No:.................................... (If applicable) and complete the name and address details below. Alternatively, these books are available from many local Newsagents including W.H.Smith, J.Menzies, Martins and other paperback stockists from 14th May 1993.

Name:...

Address:..

....Post Code:..........................

To Retailer: If you would like to stock M&B books please contact your regular book/magazine wholesaler for details.

You may be mailed with offers from other reputable companies as a result of this application.
If you would rather not take advantage of these opportunities please tick box ☐